Mind Bridges

Seven Facets of Magic

Julia H. West

Callihoo Publishing

Callihoo Publishing
P. O. Box 18481
Salt Lake City, UT 84118-0481
http://callihoo.com

Also available on Kindle and other devices

First printing July 2013

Printed in the United States of America

ISBN 978-0615840994

Contents

Preface

Through the fabric of all the cultures of our world there runs a thread of magic. This belief in magic transcends race, color, religion, and nationality. Even those who profess not to believe in magic are often fascinated by fantasy tales of its use.

The working of magic is different in Europe and Japan, or amongst the Inuit, or Nigerians, or any of thousands of other peoples on our planet. Some magic requires chanting and spells, other workings use animal sacrifice, sand painting, or fasting. The rituals and implements vary as widely as the cultures that use them.

As I studied for my degree in anthropology, I read about many different magic systems, past and present. I haven't used any systems verbatim in the stories in this collection, but elements of magical beliefs, as well as other fascinating details of people's lives, make their way into many of my tales. The rest is purely the product of my imagination.

The common thread between all these stories is their magic. From the paintings in "Soul Walls" through the spell baths in "Strength, Wisdom, and Compassion" to the string figures in "Power Sources," these stories explore different facets of magic, and how that magic affects the people who use it—and those it is used upon.

The ideas for each of the magic systems in the stories came from different sources. For "Gathering Shards" I read a paragraph in a *Lark in the Morning* catalog describing Tibetan Tingsha. "Traditionally, these miniature cymbals are struck to call 'hungry ghosts' to accept offerings. By relieving their hunger and making an offering, their suffering is diminished and only when all suffering is eliminated can enlightenment be achieved." Within an hour of reading this description, I had an outline for the story.

For "Strength, Wisdom, and Compassion" I pondered the best way to put a lasting spell upon someone. Wouldn't submerging a person in bespelled water, so the magic could be drawn in through the person's pores, strengthen the spell and make it act more quickly, with a stronger overall effect?

My inspiration for "Not the Best Neighbors" was a picture of a beautifully engraved metal needlecase from the Middle Ages. I wanted the heroine to use it in an unorthodox way. The magic in this story is of the 'wizard casting spells' variety common to many modern fantasy stories.

When I was a teenager, in college for the first time, I wrote a research paper on string figures. I was fascinated by the fact that some figures created with the exact same moves had been devised by cultures half a world apart, with no possible contact between the cultures. Could it be there was some underlying 'rightness' about certain figures, that each culture discovered them because of their inherent magic? For decades, the idea of using string figures as magic lurked in the back of my mind. When I finally used the idea, in "Power Sources," it was in a science fiction setting—another planet—and the aliens were those who created the magic. My early voracious reading of the works of Andre Norton gave me a great love for mixing science fiction—spaceships and aliens—with fantasy in my own writing.

For "Soul Walls," I used research for a science fiction novel I'm writing, on Hopi culture. Running was very important to early cultures in southwestern America. The people in my story are not Hopi, but were based on the culture. The concept of soul walls themselves is my own idea, though the idea fits well with the culture I built, and the tendency of many cultures to record important events in caves or on stone walls.

In "Changes of Life" I wanted to turn the common theme of a girl finding her magical powers at puberty—as she becomes a woman—on its head. What if magic doesn't manifest until a woman reaches the other end of her reproductive life: menopause? A life spent gaining knowledge and wisdom would be capped by learning to control magic.

I'm not sure why I've explored the concept of blindness in several stories—perhaps because I'm quite nearsighted, and eyesight is very precious to me as a reader and writer. In "Skin and Bones" I posit a group of people who, perhaps by magic, perhaps by mutation, can see in the dark. In their damp underground caves, 'normal' sighted folks are blind.

These seven stories only scratch the surface of what can be done with magic systems. The power of the human mind is incredible. The authors of fantasy stories harness that power to create stories that not only entertain with their details, but delve into the depths of the mind to describe eternal truths through use of the fantastic. These stories bridge the gap between the mundane world and that of fantasy. Welcome to the Mind Bridge.

Julia H. West
June 2013
West Jordan, Utah

Soul Walls

Tiva and the other apprentices sat cross-legged on mats in front of Yongosona's house, eating rolled corn cakes and enjoying the dawn breeze teasing the mesa top. Behind them the sun rose, its rays painting Red Cliff, far to the west. Already the air was hot, and they'd been up since before dawn, plastering the wall at Chumana's house, so the breeze was doubly welcome.

Yongosona, their teacher, pushed the woven door hanging aside and stepped out into the sand outside her door. She was an old woman, the oldest Tiva had ever seen—wrinkled and stooped, her hair wispy as summer clouds—but was still bright of eye and steady of hand. Her fingers, tunic and skirt were all daubed with the paints of her profession.

Paints, Tiva thought in dissatisfaction. *I run half a day to collect materials for them, I grind them, I mix them—but I never get to* use *them.*

"Today," Yongosona said, "we paint Chumana's Soul Wall."

Tiva glanced up at her teacher. Yongosona usually did not say 'we' when she spoke of painting. Would she allow one—or several—of her apprentices to aid her in more than plastering walls or mixing paint this day? Tiva pushed the rest of her corn cake into her mouth, dusted her hands off on her skirt, and rose to her feet.

The other apprentices also stood, from Honovi—already a woman and looking forward to when her own Soul Wall would be painted—to little Pamuya, who was in her eighth summer and had come to Yongosona at winter's end.

Yongosona gazed up at the girls for a long time, never blinking. Her gaze was distant; she was thinking of the Soul Wall to be painted. Finally she said, "Honovi, bring the gold earth and the white. Tiva, the most brilliant red and the black. Kawaina, all the greens. Lomahansi, the light blue . . . and the jewel blue. Pamuya, carry the basket of brushes and scrapers."

The girls scrambled into Yongosona's house. The inside back wall was covered with shelves which held pots and carved stone boxes, and pegs from which baskets and tight-woven bags depended. By now all the girls, even Pamuya, knew exactly where every piece of Yongosona's equipment belonged.

Tiva took down the pot of brightest red paint. She lifted the lid and peered inside. There was little left—Yongosona had used much bright red in the last Soul Wall. Maybe that would be enough; it seemed this wall would have much green and blue in it.

She put that pot and the larger one of black paint in a small basket, padding the pots with straw so they wouldn't strike against each other and break. Usually she had much more to carry. Yongosona always took an apprentice with her when she painted a Soul Wall, but most of the girls were sent off on errands, or stayed at Yongosona's house making paint. Excitement rose in Tiva's chest. They were all going today!

The girls followed their teacher along the plateau, through sandy lanes between attached houses plastered in brown, cream, and red. Chumana's brothers and other kinsmen had just finished adding her new home to her mother's, and were plastering it in the same warm orange-red shade.

The men stopped their work and stood aside, nodding and murmuring "Grandmother" as Yongosona and her apprentices passed into the house. It did not have a door hanging yet; that was still on Chumana's intended husband's loom, a day at least from completion.

Tiva, standing in the doorway, saw a half-grown boy, Chumana's brother, run into his mother's house. Moments later, Chumana and her husband-to-be came out, faces shining with excitement. Chumana carried an armload of cushions; Honovi accepted one from her and helped Yongosona to seat herself cross-legged on it, then the apprentices all lined up behind their teacher, still holding their burdens.

"Esteemed elder," Chumana said, touching her forehead at Yongosona. Mikwliya, her husband-to-be, echoed her.

"Sit." Yongosona motioned to the floor in front of her. They dropped cushions and sat before her, side by side, shoulders touching. Yongosona reached out, the loose sleeves of her multi-colored tunic falling back as she spread her fingers and rested them on the foreheads of the young couple before her. All three closed their eyes.

Tiva quietly pulled the straw from the basket she carried. Beside her, she felt Honovi doing the same. They never knew how long this part would take, but when Yongosona asked for paint it must be ready to set into her hand.

Yongosona took a long time. Pamuya fidgeted, shifting her weight from one foot to the other. Yongosona's arms were shaking now, and sweat ran down the faces of the young couple.

Yongosona began to hum, a monotonous up-and-down sound. Tiva wished she knew what Yongosona was doing. Somehow, she was discovering what to paint on the Soul Wall, but she would never tell her apprentices *how* she knew. Was it something only in her mind? Did a god tell her? How could Tiva ever paint Soul Walls if she never got to paint and didn't know *what* to paint?

Abruptly Yongosona dropped her arms and opened her eyes. "Go," she told Chumana and Mikwliya.

Chumana—only two summers older than Tiva—staggered to her feet and pulled Mikwliya up with her. Without a word, they left the house.

Tiva and Honovi helped Yongosona to her feet. The old woman took a paintbrush from the basket Pamuya held and stood surveying the wall they had prepared that morning, blank white. She gestured with the brush, then said, "Red."

Tiva took the lid off the red pot and placed it under Yongosona's brush. What did the old woman see as she surveyed the unblemished wall before her? Did the painting live behind her eyes, merely needing to be copied onto the surface? And how had she known before she came what colors she would need?

One long curving line, then another, red on the white surface. Then, "Black." Tiva held out the other pot, and Yongosona took another brush from Pamuya.

Tiva watched carefully. She knew that at this stage in Yongosona's Soul Walls there was no discernable design. Tiva couldn't look at a section and say, "This will be a spine tree, this will be a gazelope." But later, when it was nearly finished, all the various parts came together, and she would be able to see that this black line was the gazelope's hip, and that brown one traced an eagle's wing.

Today, it seemed, Yongosona would *tell* them what her lines meant. She began to murmur as she painted, and Tiva had to listen hard to understand. "Swiftness for their children, like the sandrat over the desert," she said as a line in gold earth, then a few more, became a sandrat's supple length. Tiva's heart began to pound. Yongosona was explaining what she painted! She had done this seldom since Tiva became her apprentice.

The other girls didn't seem to notice. They held paints for their teacher and Pamuya clutched used brushes. They fidgeted and yawned as the painting grew before their eyes and Yongosona's voice, quiet as a breeze, described sandrose and corn stalk.

Then Yongosona said "red" once more, but instead of dipping her brush into the pot, she squinted at it. "Not enough brilliant red," she said. "Need more tomorrow." She looked up at Tiva. "Go to Red Cliff now. Get the brightest red earth."

She turned away from Tiva, asked for green, took another brush, and traced a line—part of a cornstalk—close to one of earth gold.

Though she wanted to stay and listen to Yongosona's explanations, Tiva set her pots down next to Honovi and ran out the door. She held her hand up to gauge how high the sun stood above the village. It was already a few handwidths above the horizon. Red Cliff was half a day's run away, and after she gathered the earth she would need time for grinding and mixing the pigment. She must make the most of the daylight.

She hardly paused when she reached Yongosona's house. Food bags hung, already filled, on their pegs. Water bag here, basket for the earth she would collect here. Already on the run, she dropped the bags into the basket and left the house's dark coolness for sunlight as she settled the basket on her back.

The path from the mesa to the desert below was steep and zigzagged down the cliff side. But the men and boys who ran it every day to get to their fields below had pounded it hard and smooth with their feet, and Tiva sped up. She was getting her stride now, and only slowed a little at each turn for the next long downward slant. She ignored the dizzying drop an arm's length to one side.

Red Cliff, as far west as Tiva had ever been in her sixteen summers, was the western border of the land claimed by Tiva's village, Ayantavi. They shared it with their neighbor to the north, Shokitevela. The boundaries had been negotiated between their Talker Chiefs generations before, since both villages obtained earth for pigment at Red Cliff.

When she reached the desert floor, Tiva settled into a steady pace, running with a long stride. She had learned that if she *tried* to run fast, she just tired herself. So she ran, her face toward Red Cliff, her thoughts wandering far from the desert she traversed.

Yongosona would not let her paint, but that did not mean Tiva did not paint. Red Cliff had many caves and there was one—far up the cliff, a hard scramble—where she had smoothed and plastered the wall and sometimes tried painting for herself. But her lines were wobbly, and no matter what curves and lines she added, she rarely saw a plant or animal. She had plastered over many attempts, but was beginning to think she would end up like many of Yongosona's other apprentices. She would find a nice boy in another village and bring him home, and Yongosona would paint them a Soul Wall, and she would turn to decorating pottery or making patterns for weaving.

Red Cliff was closer now, and Tiva sipped from her water bag, never breaking stride. She adjusted her headscarf so the sun, directly overhead, wouldn't burn the back of her neck. The basket on her back was beginning to chafe through her sweat-damp tunic. When she stopped, she'd adjust it.

The desert, under the mid-day sun, was quiet. Animals were smarter than humans, and hid in their cool dens when the sun was fiercest. Always running, breathing deeply but without panting, Tiva surveyed the area. Yellow sand everywhere, dotted with grey-green brush, and now and then a darker rock poking through. Nothing moved, no breeze stirred the sparse branches; even the dust of her running sank almost immediately. She was alone with her discontent.

Yongosona had been explaining today, had told them things as she worked. Usually she merely grunted words—requesting paints, brushes, or other materials. What were the others learning while Tiva was off gathering earth? In eight summers of helping Yongosona, Tiva could count the times when the old woman had explained her paintings on the fingers of one hand. Yongosona taught them to make the materials, and then bade them watch and think on what they saw.

Tiva watched, and Tiva thought. But she had not learned how to paint. She had not learned what made a Soul Wall the heart of a home, and not just a decoration like she could paint on a pot.

"You run well, girl," said a voice close to her ear.

Almost, she broke her stride. Almost, she stumbled. But she caught herself and stared, open-mouthed and startled, at the young man running beside her. He must have been resting in the scant shadow of one of the rocks, or she would have seen him earlier. Now he paced her easily, running alongside and grinning at her shock.

"Thank you," she said finally. "I have far to go."

"You do," he said, his words smooth, his breathing easy, though he ran as swiftly as she. "May I run with you?"

His face had a familiar look to it. Like the runners in Shokitevela, he had his waist-length hair tied with a cloth striped in red and yellow, but his trousers and tunic were white, not bright colored as most men favored. Perhaps she had seen him before, at the races with Shokitevela last fall. There should be no harm in his running alongside her. "If you wish," she answered.

They ran together, the only sound their sandals swishing through the sand and the slight *huff, huff* of their breathing. Soon the young man's silence began to disturb Tiva. Why did he want to run with her, if he had nothing to say? Did he wish to spy out where Ayantavi got their colored earths, to take them for his own village? Men did not paint, but they did weave, and the brilliant red earth would color his yarn far better than the faded red in his head-cloth. She began to regret allowing him to run alongside her.

"Sensing souls is difficult," he said, startling her from her uneasy thoughts.

"Yes," she said, to cover her renewed shock. "I . . . I don't know if I have the right soul to sense those of others." Why had she told him that? It was her most private fear, one she had told no one else, and now she had blurted it to a stranger.

"You try too hard and not hard enough." He said the words casually, as if he knew her, as if he were not a stranger from another village, with no business to know what she did or why.

It stung her, his response, and she answered again without thinking, "I watch, and I think. That is what I have been taught."

"What do you watch?" he asked.

What *did* she watch? Yongosona. How she mixed colors. How she drew the curves and lines. How she shaded paint into paint, how she used colors and what colors she used. What brushes she chose, which feathers and sticks she used to smooth and delineate. Tiva had watched this for eight summers, and thought she knew well enough what Yongosona did. But she still did not know *why*.

"I watch my teacher," Tiva told him, just to break the silence.

"Do you watch what she does *not* do as well as what she does?" he asked.

Why did his questions fret her so? She remembered this morning, standing bored and restless as Yongosona touched Chumana's and Mikwliya's foreheads. She had *not* watched when Yongosona was not painting. Something stirred deep in her mind. *Watch and think*.

"You have far to go," the stranger said, and his stride grew longer, his steps quicker. She lengthened her own stride to keep even with him, and he sped up even more.

"Are you a painter?" she asked, and noted with shame that her voice was breathless with the pace they were now running.

"I am a painter, yes," he said, "And more. As are you." His voice was as even and easy as it had ever been, though he ran as if he were in the fall races, sprinting to prove his village's superiority.

Her lungs were starting to feel the pace, as were the joints in her hips, knees, and ankles. Her arms pumped at her sides, as if she could thus pull herself forward through the air.

"Look to your walls," he said, and with satisfaction she heard him panting, just a bit. But then she frowned. *My walls?*

"What do you . . . mean? I'm not . . . married yet. I don't . . . have a Soul Wall." She didn't think she could run faster. She was sprinting, not pacing herself for the rest of her journey to Red Cliff. He was drawing ahead, and for some reason she could not let that happen.

"Change how you watch. Change how you think." He turned his head, grinned at her, and put on a greater burst of speed.

She could not keep up. He must be his village's champion runner, sent out to gather earth from Red Cliff for his village. He had seen her, and chosen to tease her on his way. Regaining her normal pace, she fought gasping breaths back to steadiness. He ran on toward the cliff until sight of his dark hair and white clothing was lost in the desert's heat shimmer.

Now Tiva slowed for a moment, to adjust her headscarf, smooth the wrinkle out of her tunic where the basket rode on her shoulders, and take another sip of water. She had allowed herself to become overheated; that was bad. Her tunic was soaked with sweat, and her skirt flapped clammily about her calves.

What had he been saying to her? Change her way of watching and thinking? Again something—an idea—flickered in the back of her mind, but she could not catch it. She set out again, in her accustomed stride, and slowly the ache eased itself from calves and hips, and her throat ceased burning.

Red Cliff was much closer than she had expected. How far had she run while sprinting against the unknown man? The ground underfoot changed, from yellow-white sand to gray earth streaked with red. There were more stones here, and she had to watch her footing, not lose herself in thinking.

At the cliff's base she paused, shading her eyes with a hand to peer at the sun. She had gotten here more rapidly than anticipated. If she dug her red earth quickly she might have time to practice painting.

Practice painting. What could she change, to make her paintings better? Always before she had painted as Yongosona did—starting with bold lines and working from them. But what if painting worked differently for her? She had never tried painting what felt right for *her*; she had always tried to emulate her teacher. Was that what the young man had meant, when he said, 'Change how you watch, change how you think'?

Excitement swept through Tiva. She wanted to try it *now*, try to paint with her own eyes and mind, not Yongosona's. She ran down the long cliff, away from where most of the apprentices collected red earth. Then she scrambled up the wind-carved stone face, fingers and sandaled feet finding places easily. She had often wished that she didn't have to paint the way Yongosona did. But she had pushed that desire away, thinking she *had* to paint like her teacher. But if she *changed* her thinking. . . .

The cave was cooler, out of the direct sunlight. She didn't have time to plaster the wall, didn't have many pre-mixed paints available, but it didn't matter. Today she wanted to try something different, to . . . to *experiment*. Her heart beat against her ribs, and she laughed breathlessly. To get so excited about something she did every day of her life. It was only painting, after all.

But today it wasn't *only* painting. In fact, she didn't even open the tightly covered paint pots hidden in a niche. Instead, she took a charred stick and stood before the fresh white wall, the wall she had covered over so ferociously after her last failed attempt.

Think. *Change* the way you think. Instead of drawing a line and expecting the painting to emerge from it, think first of what should be there. Cornstalks in her father's fields, heavy heads waving in a slight evening breeze? Her mother's cat, curled in the exact center of a woven rug with an expression of extreme satisfaction? Her youngest brother, half-asleep against his father, one finger in his mouth as he listened to the evening tales? All these things were part of her family's soul.

Is this how Yongosona knew what to paint on a Soul Wall? But Tiva's thoughts were of how her family was *now*. How could she draw what was to come? How could she draw a family's destiny before the family was even begun?

Change the way you think. Yongosona had lived in Ayantavi, and painted Soul Walls, since Tiva's grandmother was a girl. She knew everyone, had watched children be born and grow. She had seen boys leave for other villages, had seen girls bring in their excited young husbands-to-be. Yongosona's husband was dead, and her sons lived in other villages. Was the whole village now her family, so she could see into their souls as Tiva could see her own parents and brothers? But what about the boys marrying in? Yongosona couldn't know their souls. She had not watched them grow up, did not know if they were smart or lazy or rambunctious.

Tiva shook her head. Too much to think on. She'd never paint anything if she thought too much. So for now, a painting of something she knew, and knew well. The little peach tree outside the front door of her house. It was near the end of its life, but its gnarled branches yielded the sweetest peaches in the village.

She closed her eyes and smiled. She pictured the curve of the tree's trunk, the way one side was uneven where her brother had hung on a branch and broken it off. Now it was in full leaf, and the peaches hung heavy, nearly ripe. Her father had propped the branches up with forked sticks. That curve—the branch, the twigs, the leaves. . . .

The curve she drew on the white wall wasn't wobbly or aimless, and the next curve, although making the branch thicker than it was in real life, was pleasing. She sketched on, adding hints of leaves here and there, shading fat peaches with her thumb. When she finally stood back and looked at her work, excitement gripped her again. Here was the first thing she had ever made that looked real, that looked as she thought it should. And she had done it merely by changing her thought. What power in the grinning young man's suggestion.

She shivered a little—not from cold, but from the force of what had just taken her over. Then she looked up in alarm. It was cooler in the little cave than it had been. The sun was behind Red Cliff now, and the day was passing quickly. She had still to find her red earth and get back to Ayantavi.

Assuring herself her basket was in place, she backed carefully down the hand- and footholds in the stone. The best, the brightest red earth was at the northern end of the cliff, near Shokitevela's territory.

Tiva jogged along the cliff's base, searching out the veins of bright red in the ochre and gray. There—near the ground. It was very trampled here—the other girls must come here often. She dug at the darker earth with her wooden paddle, and found there was very little bright red. She packed what she had dug into her basket and covered it with straw, then ran on along the cliff side.

She found one other place, also very trampled, that had a small amount of brilliant red. Had Yongosona used so much of it lately that her apprentices had dug up all the easy-to-find earth? A glance behind her at the cliff's long shadow told her she had little time to find enough and begin her long run home.

The ground began to rise, and Tiva saw only gray stone for stride after stride. She had come too far north; she would have to turn around and see if she had missed other places to dig the brilliant red. But no—there, just above head height on the side of the cliff, where scattered stone showed a bit of the wall had fallen recently, was more of the brilliant red she sought.

Tiva headed for it eagerly, but then stopped and looked around. She *had* come too far north. She was in Shokitevela's territory. This was their earth. She couldn't take what didn't belong to her village. She stopped, irresolute. The cliff's shadow spread far across the desert now, the sun long past its zenith. She had so little time to find more earth, get back to the village, and prepare the paint this night for tomorrow's painting. Would Shokitevela begrudge her a basketful of earth? There were no footprints—it seemed Shokitevela's painters had not come here. And the vein was large—she could see that.

She stooped to gather stones that had fallen from the cliff face, to pile them up to stand on so she could reach the red earth above. A lizard ran out from under one and raised its head, gazing at her. She stared back. Usually lizards were so shy of people that the whisk of a tail and tiny footprints in the sand were all she ever saw. This one sat still, just out of reach, its bright black eyes staring. It was beautiful, its sand-gold hide beaded with black and tan and banded with red. Its sides expanded and contracted as it breathed, and it gazed at her as steadfastly as she stared at it.

"Kukutsi," she breathed. This lizard was sacred to Shokitevela. She knew, seeing it here, that she was *not* to take their earth, no matter how great she thought her need. She let her head drop. "Yes, Kukutsi. I will leave."

Kukutsi turned its head, surveying her with each bright eye in turn, then whisked out across the sand.

Tiva took a deep breath, released it, then ran back the way she had come.

Back in her own territory, there was a little more brilliant red earth far above her head; she found hand and footholds, but had to hook her basket over one arm—very awkward. Added to what she already had, the basket was less than half full. But it would have to do; the cliff's shadow reached so far across the desert now that the sun must be little more than a few hands above the western horizon. Tiva packed the earth carefully, drank more water, and pulled out a corn cake to nibble. In her earlier excitement to paint, she had forgotten to eat.

She started back through the rougher ground east of the cliff, stumbling occasionally. She was tired now, and the journey back to Ayantavi seemed almost more than she could accomplish. She took another sip and stretched her legs, knowing she must not delay.

She ran out of the cliff's long shadow into late afternoon heat. She was surprised to see another runner heading out from the cliff, angling more to the north and already farther east than she was.

The runner saw her and slowed. Tiva put on a burst of speed and soon was running alongside the other girl. It was Nakwanpa, one of the apprentices to Koloh-Pohu, Shokitevela's Soul Wall painter.

"You are out late," Nakwanpa said, rather breathless.

"As are you," Tiva returned. "Your village is farther from here than mine—you've a long run ahead of you."

Nakwanpa ran quietly for a moment, then answered, "I sought the brightest red earth and found little. I stayed overlong in the search."

"Ah, then we are alike!" said Tiva. "I, too, was looking for brilliant red, but the veins are almost used up." She stopped there. Should she tell Nakwanpa of the large new vein she had found in Shokitevela's territory? To do so would admit she had gone beyond Ayantavi's boundary. But it had been an honest error, and she'd taken nothing.

"I searched so far up Red Cliff that I strayed into your territory," Tiva admitted. "At the north end of the cliffs, where the ground rises, there is new-fallen stone. A large vein of brilliant red was uncovered."

Nakwanpa turned her head to Tiva, a smile wreathing her dusty features. "Thank you, Tiva, for telling me this. May your painting go well." The other girl sped up, angling north again. Just before she was out of earshot, she turned her head and called, "In your territory, halfway back along the cliff, there is a crevice with three sandrose bushes at its mouth. Follow it back and see if the brilliant red is as plentiful as it looked from its mouth."

Tiva waved her thanks and ran on, her spirit lighter. Each had found red earth in the other's territory. She thought Nakwanpa hadn't entered the cleft, hadn't taken any earth from Ayantavi's territory. She was doubly glad she had not dug any of Shokitevela's earth.

It was nearly dark when Tiva ran the last long path up the cliff and reached her village. The smell of savory sauces cooking made her stomach growl. Cheerful voices rang over the plateau as families gathered at the day's end. But she could not go to her family yet; she must bring her basket to Yongosona.

Yongosona sat on a mat outside her house grinding pigment in a stone mortar, lamps flickering in niches to either side of her. She looked up as Tiva, panting from the effort of the last long climb to the village, halted. "Late."

"Yes, Grandmother," Tiva said, bowing her head. "The sources of brilliant red are almost used up."

The old woman held out her hands for Tiva's basket. Without looking inside, she weighed it in her palms. Her face seemed to sag into more wrinkles than usual.

"There was more," Tiva blurted. "But I found it after I wandered into Shokitevela's territory. I . . . did not think it would be good to take their earth."

Yongosona looked up at Tiva, reflections of the lamp flames dancing in her eyes. She studied the girl for a long time, as Tiva tried very hard not to fidget. Tiva's mouth grew dry, and sweat broke out on her brow despite the cool evening breeze.

The old woman said finally, "Shokitevela's earth would not suit an Ayantavi Soul Wall." She handed the basket back to Tiva. "All will be needed."

Tiva took the basket, pushed the doorflap aside, and hurried into Yongosona's house for another mortar, to grind the red earth for tomorrow's paint. As she settled down beside Yongosona, she tried not to feel the hollowness of her stomach and the aches in shoulders and legs.

Tiva was up before the dawn with the other apprentices, preparing new plaster for Chumana's Soul Wall. She had not slept well, and her calves still ached, but the brilliant red had all been ground and mixed. It rested now in covered pots, ready for Yongosona's use.

The plastering complete, they all ate, and Yongosona assigned them tasks. Tiva was sent off to Dry Gorge to gather insects for bright blue paint. Tiva wasn't sure if Yongosona had assigned her this task because she was displeased with her performance of the day before or not. Dry Gorge was much closer to Ayantavi than Red Cliff, but gathering gembugs was an unpleasant chore.

Tiva took a tight-woven bag as well as the carry basket, for gembugs were small and sifted through basket mesh or the weave of normal cloth. She set off quickly. Today she would make Yongosona proud of her. She knew where the best spine trees were, and should be able to gather many gembugs and be home long before dusk.

The air was still and hot as Tiva raced down the path to the desert below the village. The little hairs on her arms crawled, and Tiva scanned the sky for clouds. It felt like thunderstorm weather.

As she ran, the uneasy feeling that someone was watching plagued her. She often scanned the terrain ahead, looking for telltale puffs of dust from running feet. No one. It must be the tickly, itchy feeling of the air.

Dry Gorge was a long, deep crack in the ground, empty of water most of the time. In the spring, snow melted in the far-off mountains and filled the gorge with roiling muddy water. The only other time water flowed in the gorge was when it rained heavily in those same mountains, sending water down the gorge even when the desert got no rain at all. The thunderstorm feel in the air made Tiva cautious.

There was a path worn into Dry Gorge's steep side. She traversed it carefully; it was not as hard-packed and reliable as the one down the cliff back at home, for most of it was destroyed every spring. Once on the gorge's pebbled floor, she trotted down the relatively clear ways between spine trees, candleplants, and sandrose.

Many plants grew here, for there was water far below the ground. The oldest spine trees had roots that must reach halfway through the world, searching for water. They were so well rooted that even flash floods did not dislodge them. These elder trees were the best places to seek gembugs.

Tiva found the huge, many-branched spine tree she sought. It was so tall its highest branches could be seen above the lip of the gorge, almost the same yellow-brown as the sand. The tree was so old that Yongosona had sought gembugs here when *she* was an apprentice. Spines longer than Tiva's middle finger grew from trunk, branches, and twigs. They were sharp, and their sap made any scratch or puncture itch and swell.

It was easy to tell where gembugs had made their homes in the tree. Whenever a spine tree was damaged, spines grew like bristling whiskers from the wound.

The first bristly area Tiva found was in the trunk, just above head height. She wrapped her arm in a piece of leather and carefully angled her hand, holding a stone knife, in toward the swollen area where the gembugs lived. It was awkward, as she couldn't see above her head. Spines brushed the leather around her wrist, but she kept them from puncturing through it.

She got her knife to the base of the swollen area, and was startled by a sharp chittering noise. A sandrat poked its slender nose out of the hole in the spine tree's trunk and cursed at her. Tiva froze in place, not wanting to get scratched by the spines, but also wary of the sandrat's teeth. So this wasn't a gembug nest, but a sandrat den! She didn't remember seeing sandrats nesting in the spine trees before. Again, she had not been watching, or had watched the wrong things. She needed to remember what the young man had told her yesterday: *Change how you watch.*

"Carefully now, little sister, Tuwakala," Tiva told the sandrat. "I will leave your house alone." The sandrat pulled all but the tip of its nose back into its den, and Tiva snaked her hand out from among the spines. "I will go elsewhere to hunt insects."

She circled the tree, looking for more bristly spots. There was one as high as she could reach, but it would be too hard to get past the spines and cut out the insect nest at the end of her reach. Finally, she chose a small nest on a branch about chest height. As she cut the nest away and dropped it into her bag, she heard a cracking sound above her.

A sandrat—perhaps the one she had seen before—stood perched on one of the largest spines. Its long slender arms and hand-like paws were perfect for reaching past the short bristles of spines and into a gembug nest high above Tiva's head. The rat cracked a gembug between its teeth, then dropped the jewel-like carapace into the sand at the base of the spine tree.

Tiva dropped to her knees in the coarse dirt. It was littered with gembug carapaces. Why had she never noticed this before? The bright blue gembug armor glittered in the sunlight like tiny jewels. She scooped them up, dirt and all, into her sack. She could winnow them like grass seed to remove the dirt.

The sandrat chittered above her. "Thank you, Tuwakala," Tiva said. She followed the rat as it moved around the spine tree trunk, found another gembug nest, and started cracking more insects open.

A low rumble rolled over the desert, and both girl and sandrat paused to peer at the sky. Clouds had rolled in while Tiva had been occupied gathering gembugs, and now it seemed the thunderstorm that Tiva had felt earlier had arrived, unnoticed.

Quickly, Tiva scooped as much of the gembug-bright dirt from underneath the tree as she could, then tied the bag securely shut and lashed it into her basket. If the thunderstorm was here now, had it rained earlier in the mountains? She had not thought to watch, to notice if there were clouds over the mountains.

She started up the narrow, dusty trail, then paused when the sandrat chittered. The low rumble of thunder came again, louder. The sandrat had run to the doorway of its den and hung outside it, clutching a long spine and scolding at the noise.

Tiva realized that if a flash flood did come down Dry Gorge, the tree would survive the crushing force of the water, but the sandrat's home would be flooded. Did the rat have babies in its den? Would it come with her? Heartbeats later she stood beneath the tree once more, reaching up into the den. "Tuwakala, help me save your babies," she told the anxiously chittering sandrat. "I can't see into your den."

Did the sandrat hear? Did it understand? Tiva felt something warm and wriggly beneath her hand, picked it up, and transferred a sandrat no longer than her little finger into her basket. Another, then another, until seven squeaking youngsters crawled over one another in her basket. An adult—the father?—leaped from the mouth of the den to her basket, followed by the original sandrat, who had seemingly been keeping watch, clinging to a long spine halfway up the tree.

Tiva raced now for the path. There was another rumbling, not the thunder that accompanied the clouds. Tiva risked a look up the gorge, then turned back to watch her footing in the treacherous gravel. She couldn't see anything yet, but the noise grew ever louder. Higher she climbed, glancing nervously backward every few steps. Then she saw it—a wall of water, dirty brown and full of sticks and stones—thundering down the gorge toward her.

She stopped looking back, spent all her energy scrambling up the chancy path. In her basket, the sandrats were quiet now, and she couldn't even feel them moving. Were they as scared as she? Heart pounding, she used hands and feet to drag herself up.

She was almost to the top when a hand reached down and pulled her over the gorge's rim and into gusting wind. She stood, breathing hard, staring down at the murky depths of the water racing through the gorge.

"Thank you," she said when she had caught her breath and was no longer trembling with fright. She turned to see who had helped her.

It was a woman, middle-aged, plump and rosy cheeked. Her headscarf was woven in green and brown zigzags, her tunic was green, and her skirt, whipped against her legs by storm winds, was brown. No village that Tiva knew used those colors.

"You're a long way from home," the woman said, helping Tiva brush dirt from her skirt.

"I came for the gembugs," Tiva said simply. All the villages shared Dry Gorge, for it was the best source anywhere for gembugs and other creatures—plant and animal—that thrived between its walls.

"So I see," the woman said, smiling. "And do you also gather sandrats?"

"Ah. No, I was saving them from the flood. Mama rat was cracking gembugs for me. . . ." she trailed off. That sounded absurd, even though it had seemed, at the time, as if that was exactly what was happening.

"I am sure they are grateful not to be down in that." The woman indicated the roiling water below them with a nod.

"Ye-yes." Tiva watched the water with a little shiver of horror. What if she hadn't made it up the path quickly enough? Whole trees floated down the once-dry gorge, smashing into the walls with the water's force. The flood hadn't reached the top of the great spine tree, but Tiva was sure the sandrats could not have carried their babies up the trunk in time.

"You were watching well today," the woman told her.

Tiva stared at her. The young man yesterday had spoken of watching. It was because of his words that she had noticed the gembug carapaces glittering in the dirt. But she had almost let the flash flood take her because she hadn't been paying attention to the sky. "Not as well as I could have," she muttered.

Thunder rumbled, and Tiva looked up at shining gray clouds hurrying across the sky, sped on by the wind that threatened to pull her headscarf off. "I need to get home," she said.

"As do they." The woman waved a hand at Tiva's basket.

"Oh, the sandrats." Tiva looked around. There were spine trees here, gnarled by wind and lack of water. Strong trees, survivors in a way different from those in the gorge bottom. When she walked over to inspect one, one of the adult sandrats leaped from the basket to a branch. It ran along the branch, avoiding spines the length of its body with ease. At the trunk it paused, then scampered upward. Around the trunk, along another branch, it explored the tree from top to bottom.

It stopped at a whiskery growth tucked between the trunk and the base of a branch. Twisting its long, supple body around the spines, it reached a paw into the nest and brought forth gembugs to crunch. It chittered, and the other adult sandrat followed it to the nest. Tiva watched in fascination as the two opened up the gembug nest and made themselves a hole to hide in. In the doing they spilled what must be generations of gembug carapaces into the sand at the tree's base.

"Little brother, little sister—Tuwakala—do you want your babies there?"

The response of the longer, yellower of the pair—the mother, Tiva thought—was to reach out a slender paw and chitter some more. Tiva took her basket off her back and, one by one, transferred the squirming, squeaking youngsters from the folds of the sheltering sack into the hole.

When they were all in she thought for a moment, then pulled the headscarf off her head. Storm wind whipped hair into her face, but she ignored that and handed the fabric to the sandrat. "To soften your new nest," she said. It was appropriate, she thought, for the blue stripes in the scarf came from gembug dye. The sandrat took the scarf and pulled it into the hole, blocking the entrance so Tiva could no longer see the sandrat family.

Thunder crashed, overhead it seemed, and Tiva couldn't help cringing as she looked up. Strands of hair stung her face, and she shivered.

"A fine storm."

Tiva started. In her concern for the sandrats she'd forgotten the woman. Now she glanced over to see her standing tall, head thrown back and arms raised above her head. She'd taken off her headscarf, and released her knee-length hair from its braids, and it writhed around her like something living. Tiva wanted to hide behind the tree, spines or no. Surely this was no normal woman, but one of the gods. What would a god see in Tiva, the painter who never got to paint?

A gust tore the headscarf from the woman's hand, and Tiva seized it before it could be blown away.

"Keep that," the woman said, turning her face to the wind.

Tiva also faced into the wind, that her hair would be blown back from her face and she could tame it with the green-and-brown headscarf. What should she think, that this powerful being had given her a token?

"We must go now." The woman set off running through the desert, angling against the wind. Her destination seemed the line on the horizon that was the cliffs where Ayantavi lay.

Tiva looked at the gembug carapaces spilled beneath the spine tree, wanting to pick them up. But the woman had said they must go *now*. She could return for the gembug shells another day.

She shouldered her basket and, feet sure in the harder dirt past the gorge's lip, ran after the woman. The woman was already far ahead of her, and she pushed herself, lengthening her stride. The wind shifted, pushing at her back rather than her side, as if it would help her catch up with the woman.

Breath came easily now, the itchy thunder feeling of the air gone. The wind, damp with rain that never touched the desert floor, caressed her arms and back, helped her along, as her strides steadily shortened the distance between herself and the strange woman.

Then she was nearly even with the woman, who ran well for one so plump. "Who are you?" she called.

"A friend," the woman said, and the distance between them began to grow once more. "Who are you?"

Normally she would have answered 'Tiva of Ayantavi,' but she was certain that was not what the woman really asked. *Who am I?* She was Tiva, daughter of her parents, sister to her brothers, apprentice to Yongosona. She would be those things no matter what—they were external to her, not something inside. Who was she inside? Who was the real Tiva?

Like a gust of damp wind, the answer came. "I . . . am a painter." She ran on, then said with more conviction, "I *am* a painter." Even though she was still an apprentice, even though she had painted only one thing that satisfied her, she knew she was a painter. The conviction raced through her body and left it tingling with a feeling like the earlier thunder itch, but much stronger.

"And. . . ?" The woman was farther ahead of her again, the wind shredding her words.

"And much more," Tiva said, unable to put her feelings into words. She had pushed a doorflap in her mind aside and found a whole room of being behind it, and the things there dizzied her. There was the seeing that Honovi would never be a painter, and that the shells on the west bank of the Sikanvahu River yielded a better pigment than those on the east. There was the touch of her mother's hand on her cheek and her father's strong grip as he lifted her higher on a cliff to reach an abandoned bird nest. There was the comfort of a purring cat and the discontent of never painting a Soul Wall. This and much more swirled into a cord that tugged her forward.

As she struggled with her innerness, the woman had become a distant brown-and-green figure, moving across the desert with the grace and speed of a gazelope. Tiva pushed some of the tingling energy into her legs to strengthen her stride, and satisfaction washed through her as she gained on the woman once more. A question burned in her mind, one she thought the woman could answer.

The woman seemed to sense that Tiva approached her, and she sped up. Tiva drew breath deep into her lungs, and the muscles of her legs adjusted to a new, faster rhythm. Her arms moved easily, open-handed, at her sides, and she sucked damp storm wind into her nostrils to fuel her body.

The woman ran, and Tiva followed, gaining over time. Their speed grew, and burning began in Tiva's calves, the bones of her hips, her shoulders and back. Still she pushed to go faster, faster than she'd ever run, even in a sprint. It was harder to drag the damp air into her lungs now. In the dizziness beginning in her head, she almost lost the question she must ask. But the woman was just ahead, and in a moment would be close enough that Tiva could call out to her.

Tiva did not think the woman was running; she skimmed the ground like a low-flying eagle. Even the swiftest runners of all the villages had never raced an eagle, but now Tiva ran, ran until she could almost touch the woman's green tunic. She gasped out her question. "How . . . do . . . I . . . see . . . souls?"

The woman turned her head, and her face wore the grin Tiva had seen on the young man's face the day before.

"You have already begun," she said.

Darkness surrounded them. Tiva had not been watching where the woman led her, had just run, run with all her strength and will. The ground beneath her feet turned from the sometimes tricky desert sands to something firmer. The woman was a moving shadow among shadows, and Tiva poured everything she had left into staying with her. If she lost sight of the woman in this darkness, she would never see the harsh desert sunlight again.

Tiva ran, straining body and lungs. The walls around her—for she was in a cave now, a cave that stretched on and on—glowed with pale green and yellow designs. There was no opportunity for Tiva to look at them; she noted their existence and ran on. Have *I begun to see souls?* she asked herself as burning pain and exhaustion coursed through her body. *I do not understand Tiva; how can I understand others?*

A flicker of movement ahead in the pallid glow. The woman had disappeared into one of many openings in the cave walls. Tiva fixed her eyes on that one opening, indistinguishable from all the others, and pushed herself harder than she had yet. Pain shot up her legs, her lungs seared, but she reached the opening just as her strength failed.

The effort was as difficult as if she had pushed through a solid wall. Then something blazed through her, from aching feet to the top of her head. She stopped, swaying and gasping, then took a deep breath that wasn't desperate, that didn't struggle for acceptance in overtaxed lungs.

She was in a small cave, rounded like the inside of a pot, as she imagined the interior of the sandrat's den must look. The walls and ceiling shone in patterns and colors so bright that she had to squint to look at them. She followed the flow of a woman's hair as it became a mountain in a range of mountains that were designs on a lizard's back. But the lizard was a cornfield, and the ears of corn, blossoms on a peach tree.

One section drew her with a sharp internal sense of recognition. The painting flowed and built with the other patterns, but she felt a distinction. This was a pattern she had lived with, a pattern she had felt. The jewel-bright glowing colors shaped essence and personality in a way she could not describe, could only feel.

She stepped forward, hand out to touch that section of wall, to understand what drew her to the desert tortoise that was also a storm cloud over purple cliffs.

Someone put a brush into her outstretched hand. The strange woman's voice said, "Now is your time to paint, Tiva."

There was no paint pot, no bark on which to mix colors, no fresh plaster. There was only the brush and the wall, and clear space beside or above or within Yongosona's tortoise.

Tiva set brush to wall, drew a long curve that followed the curve of the tortoise shell but was separate, distinct. It was the same clear summer-sky blue that crushed gembug carapaces made. She filled her lungs with the odor of sandrose leaves and sun-heated sand, felt the tingle of thunder weather far away, and painted a brilliant zigzag descending from the storm clouds.

Then blue and red swirls—her dancing skirt at the spring gatherings—and the brilliant yellow taste of the special corn cakes made for ceremonies. Here her mother's voice chanting as she ground corn, and there her brother's giggle. Ochre in all the shades from brown through yellow to red built into the orphaned pup she was raising, a shaggy-coated dog herding sheep away from a cliff edge.

The peach tree, the branch she had drawn in charcoal on the wall of another cave, grew spine tree fruit and chicken eggs, then swirled into feather ferns that grew in sheltered places along the Sikanvahu River.

She sank to the cave floor exhausted, the brush lost somewhere under her skirts as she collapsed. She had not finished her painting—but how could she? She herself was barely begun. There were even places to fill in Yongosona's painting—her long life was not yet complete, and her painting, now joined with Tiva's, was vibrant yet.

"Who are you?" It was a whisper, filling the cave, sourceless.

"I am...." Tiva? A painter? Or something more? "I am everything I have ever seen or felt or thought or smelled or heard. I am the sandrats in the spine tree and the gembugs they crack between their teeth. I am thunder and flood. . . ." There was more, but no words for the storm of perception.

"Does that answer your question?" She could not see the woman whose voice filled the cavern with warmth.

Tiva did not have to speak. Her soul, its walls thinned by understanding, communed with painters who had known her village in generations past. There had to be that understanding, and it could not be taught. She had won through.

When Tiva sat up, she lay, arm across her basket, at the base of the path up to Ayantavi. Trembling, she pushed herself to her feet and settled the basket on her back. Had what she just felt, seen, done—had it been real? How could she paint with a brush that had no paint?

Whatever it had been, real or a vision from a god, it had changed her. She did not doubt, now, that she could paint. *She could paint!* Whether for Soul Walls or not, the painting had sunk beneath her skin, as much a part of her as her bones. The warmth of that knowledge buoyed her as she started up the path.

Sun rays shot from beneath storm clouds on the horizon, bathing Ayantavi in pink-gold light. Tiva jogged along the plateau to Yongosona's home, the basket on her back no burden. Yongosona looked up from where she sat grinding pigments, the light erasing her years, bringing back her youth.

"There was a storm," Yongosona stated.

"Yes. A flash flood in Dry Gorge." Tiva took the basket from her back and held it out to Yongosona.

"You remembered the warnings."

Tiva acknowledged that with a brief motion of her head, and Yongosona took the basket. She opened the bag, sifted its contents through her fingers. "Much dirt."

"I'll separate the insects out."

Yongosona set the basket aside. "Sit." Tiva dropped to the mat beside her. "Tomorrow, we finish Chumana's Soul Wall. And the next Wall—I think it will be Honovi's—*you* will paint."

It was what Tiva had wanted to do since she had come to Yongosona in her eighth summer. She should be excited, or scared. But the knowledge achieved in the cavern under the plateau filled her, radiated from her body like the last golden rays of sunlight. "I must learn her soul."

"Yes, you must."

The sun set behind Red Cliff, and thunder rumbled, muted by distance.

Not the Best Neighbors

Lady Janet, daughter of the Duke of Arbinclose, reined in her horse as a voice boomed, seemingly from nowhere, "Woe, woe, people of the kingdom of Chelming. This is the day of your doom."

Lord Henry, Janet's well-meaning but weak-chinned escort, pulled his horse up beside hers. He rested his hand on his sword hilt and called, "You there, you can't threaten Lady Janet."

As her horse stood restlessly shifting its feet, Janet looked about. No one on the road ahead or behind. None of the trees here at the edge of the fields were taller than two man-heights. Those slender trunks wouldn't hide a child, much less the deep-voiced man whose words still echoed in her ears.

The oddest thing about the situation was that this was the kingdom of Deccalia. Had he strayed a few leagues east to issue his pronouncement?

"This day will you fade from the sight of men. Know ye, people of Chelming, that this is the work of King Montgomery Alphonse Lawrence Edward the Third of Brixton, and tremble before you die. For a few moments, know the futility of resisting King Montgomery of Brixton."

Janet huffed an exasperated sigh. "You're in the wrong kingdom!" she called to whoever made the grand pronouncements. "This is Deccalia. *We're* not fighting you!"

The loud-voiced man, herald or whoever he may be, said nothing. Janet became annoyed. "Understand, lackey of King Montgomery. I'm Lady Janet, daughter of the Duke of Arbinclose, in *Deccalia*, and if you start harming our citizens you'll have our army on your ass so fast your head will spin."

"My lady!" Lord Henry chided. He drew out a handkerchief with his left hand, since his right still grasped his sword hilt. He mopped his brow and looked about, head bobbing like a swan's on his thin neck.

"He's the one threatening us," Janet replied. "Why should I mince words?" She raised her voice and addressed the unknown. "I'm serious, you know. Begone."

The deep voice began a series of odd syllables, in no language Janet could identify. "Eskthpf klintapoor m'skantflin."

"Knave! Cease this foul spell-mongering at once!" Janet called. *Had* King Montgomery started a war with Deccalia? She'd been away for a while—in Chelming, as a matter of fact—and that old windbag Montgomery could have picked a fight with King William of Deccalia while she was gone. King William would probably be just stupid enough to accept a challenge from Montgomery. That had nearly happened the time she visited Brixton and got in an argument with Prince Montgomery etc. etc. the Fourth—who was actually quite nice, away from his father.

The same hollow, echoing voice continued. Lord Henry jumped off his horse and ran up the road to inspect the nearest clump of trees. He shook his head, then returned to Janet. "I see no one. Where can he—"

"Asklefay!" bellowed the deep voice.

Janet's vision dimmed and her head swam. *I will not faint!* she told herself. Her horse sidled nervously across the road. She tried to calm the beast, and found she couldn't move. Her sight blurred, but she kept her eyes resolutely open. The oddest feeling swept over her body, like water (or maybe hundreds of ants) washing across her skin. If she could have moved, she would have shivered. Instead, she endured.

Moments later the feeling went away and sight returned. Janet blinked and felt for the reins; she seemed to have lost them. That was when she discovered she couldn't find the reins—or anything else that should have been there. She was completely naked, bare as her birth day. Chemise, petticoats, underdress, overdress, robe and cloak, all gone. Even her stockings and boots were missing. She wiggled her toes, watched their naked pinkness. *Oh my.*

She felt a momentary pang of admiration for King Montgomery. He'd hired himself one talented wizard this time. A spell that could remove everything from its victim, including (she checked) rings and necklaces. But had it also transported her elsewhere? She sat on a hard surface, billows of coarse cloth all around her, the sun warm on her bare skin.

She heard a loud whuff, like the sound a giant horse might make—and realized she *was* still on her mare. She clambered over drifts of heavy blue cloth, oceans of coarse lace, and a veritable waterfall of fine linen to peer a very long way down to the road. Admiration returned. *By all that's holy, a spell that shrinks an adult to the size of a man's hand.* King Montgomery must have beggared his kingdom to pay for *this* spell.

King Montgomery Alphonse Lawrence Edward the Third of Brixton sat astride his warhorse, grateful for the creature's stolid acceptance of the chaos around them. The wizard Searorun's horse, a few paces away, stood just as quietly, but King Montgomery was certain that was accomplished by magic.

One end of the meadow where King Montgomery's army massed was scorched, stinking of burnt manure, sulphur, and blood. He didn't think any of the cattle or sheep in the field had survived. Most of the foot soldiers had flung themselves to the ground when the demon—which Searorun had summoned—vanished in a flash of acrid smoke. Those still standing looked like they'd bolt for the forest behind them, given half a chance.

"The spell is complete," the sorcerer said, in a deep, hollow voice. He turned to King Montgomery and gestured toward the burned meadow. "As you can see, it has come at no little cost. Do you have my payment ready?"

"That was a very impressive bit of pyrotechnics," said King Montgomery, "but I have yet to see the effects of the spell. How do I know every man, woman and child in Chelming is gone, as you promised they would be?"

The sorcerer flushed, and flames seemed to flicker in his red hair. He held up a smoky glass bubble the size of a goose egg. Something alternately bright and dark crawled inside. "Here you see their souls, captured by my spell," he said in a dangerously calm voice.

King Montgomery stared at the sphere, almost convinced. Then the thought of the greater part of his treasury (all but the silver—the sorcerer didn't like silver), packed in carts waiting to leave the kingdom, strengthened him. "I'll give you half your fee now, and the rest when I see Chelming empty of all its folk."

Anger flared in Searorun's eyes, but he said merely, "Agreed."

While King Montgomery had a cart of treasure brought out for Searorun, Brixton's generals gathered the shaken troops. King Montgomery at their head, they marched off to take possession of Chelming.

Searorun rode close beside the king, the donkey pulling the heavily loaded cart following. For most of the day they rode slowly down Brixton's dusty roads. Here and there peasants in their fields straightened to stare open-mouthed at the king and his troops, then dropped to their knees in obeisance. King Montgomery smiled.

Just before dusk they reached the Chelming border. At Brixton's guardpost soldiers leapt to their feet and saluted. But there was no one on Chelming's side to acknowledge the army crossing their borders. No one at all.

Janet wasted no time bemoaning her fate. Weeping would not return her to proper size. She burrowed through the folds of her gown until she found the links of her metal belt. It lay along the horse's back in a huge circle, mostly buried in fabric. She followed it until she found the handkerchief she had tucked there this morning—fine linen, soft and tightly woven. Excellent material for a gown.

Near the handkerchief, still clipped to her belt, was her needlecase. It was a lovely piece of work—embossed silver, with a clasp now half the size of her hand. She wrestled it open and drew her sewing scissors—nearly as tall as she—from their loop. With considerable effort she clipped a neck hole from the center of her handkerchief, then drew the fabric over her head. She made a belt of several strands of sewing thread and looked down at herself, frowning. She was no longer naked, but she wasn't confident that this garb would hold up to any serious exercise.

Now to find the sorcerer. She had a score to settle with him! There must be some rule about ensorcelling the wrong people, and she'd hound him until he magicked her back to proper size. She wondered why the sorcerer had not appeared to gloat over the success of his spell. That *would* make him easier to find. Well, since he had not come to her, she would just have to find him.

Janet closed her needlecase and climbed over the heavy folds of fabric to stand near the saddle's pommel. Though her mare stood quietly eating roadside grass, every time the horse shifted her weight Janet nearly lost her balance.

How could she get the horse to move? Tales of Tom O'My Thumb flitted through her mind. Hadn't he stood in his mule's ear and shouted directions?

She clambered up the mare's mane, wrinkling her nose at the strong horsy smell. She didn't think she *could* stand in her mare's ear. But if she grasped the headstall of the bridle, she could sit on the horse's poll and look out over the forest. She squinted in all directions, but saw no triumphant sorcerer.

Janet shouted at the top of her lungs—but even to her own ears her voice wasn't very loud. The mare flicked an ear, shook her head, and nearly knocked Janet from her perch—but didn't start down the path.

Then she heard a muffled, squeaky voice from the ground. Probably *not* the sorcerer. "Lord Henry?" Janet called, staring down from her perch atop her horse's head. Ah. There, where he had been standing, was a pile of fabric—his very fashionable houppelande. Its sleeves, with embroidered dags as long as his arms (as long as his arms *had* been, that is) were not so practical for riding, but he was a bit of a popinjay.

The squeaky voice again, somewhat less muffled. A head poked out of the fabric. "What happened?" Lord Henry asked. "I couldn't get out of my boot!" He waved his arms. "And I was buried in—" At that moment he realized he wore nothing, squawked, and ducked back into the folds of fabric.

Janet let herself down the horse's mane and opened her needlecase again. "Here." She let her scissors drop near the pile of Lord Henry's clothing. "Cut something to cover yourself. I won't look."

While he was thus busy, she used all her strength to force her belt's clip open. She hooked the clip firmly onto the saddle and pushed the other end off the horse's back. The end clanked to the ground and raised a cloud of dust. "When you're decent, climb that. Oh, and bring my scissors with you."

A rather long time later, Lord Henry scrambled up the ladder formed by her belt's links. He wore a tunic, nearly ankle length, made of the tip of one of his sleeve dags with arm and head holes cut in the end.

When he was safely atop the mare, Janet got his help to push the heavy layers of her clothing off the horse's back. What a passerby would think of the piles of fabric, she did not know. She kept the belt. They would need it to dismount once they reached their destination.

"Hold onto the saddle," she told Lord Henry.

"What are you doing, my lady?" he asked breathlessly.

"I'm off to find who did this!" Grasping the headstall, she stamped her foot. The mare shied, moved in a half circle, and shook her head to remove the annoyance. Janet held on grimly until the horse settled to cropping roadside grass once more.

Janet stamped again, and the horse jumped and kicked.

"My lady!" called Lord Henry. "She'll shake us off." When the mare had settled and Janet could spare a look at him, he was rather pale.

"Have you a better idea?"

"No, my lady."

"Hold tight!" Janet called, suiting action to words. She gave the mare a good hard kick in the back of the neck.

The mare snorted, shivered her back, and sidled sideways. At Janet's next kick, the horse set off down the path at a trot, and Janet yelled, "Huzzah!" quite forgetting she was a demure young lady.

Lord Henry's horse followed her mare, and they trotted toward Chelming. At the Deccalia/Chelming border, the guards didn't even come out of their post. "Perhaps they were shrunk too," Lord Henry quavered.

"All the better for us," said Janet. "I'd hate to try to reason with a border guard when I'm smaller than his hand."

They rode on through empty fields until they came to a village. As the horses neared the first cottage, a score of tiny people ran out, jumping up and down and yelling.

Janet hadn't thought of how she'd *stop* her mare. Quickly she slid down the horse's neck and, bracing her feet on the saddle, grabbed the mane and pulled as hard as she could.

The mare took a few more steps, then stopped as Janet kept yanking on her mane. The people ran forward, wary of the horses' hooves, all yelling at once.

"One at a time, one at a time!" Janet called. A woman—probably tall and strong when she was her proper size—hushed the rest and stepped forward. She wore a knitted stocking.

"Do you know what happened?" the woman asked. "We heard a

voice saying 'Woe, woe, people of Chelming,' and then we shrank. Everyone in the village—"

"As far as I know, everyone in the kingdom is hand-high now," Janet interrupted. "And I want to do something about it. Will you join me?"

"What can we do?" said the woman. "We're just peasants, and smaller than kittens."

"Even kittens have claws and teeth," said Janet. "Think of what damage a horde of locusts, or a swarm of rats, can do. We just have to think like . . . rats."

Janet's and Lord Henry's horses were starting to tire, with most of the inhabitants of seven villages sitting on them, when they came across a muddle of horses in the middle of the road.

"Halt!" a tiny voice called. Janet's mare was getting used to her mane-pulling signals, and stopped when Janet wanted her to. Janet shushed the whispers of the villagers behind her, and called, "What do you want?"

A tiny man standing on the saddle of a white warhorse said, "Who are you?"

"I am Lady Janet, daughter of the Duke of Arbinclose. Who are you?"

"Captain Patterson of the Chelming army. Arbinclose is in Deccalia. What are you doing here—and why are you . . . like us?"

"I, too, crave the answer to the last question," Janet replied. "As for the first, I'm finding the sorcerer who did this, and making him change us back. These people," Janet waved at two horses full of villagers, "are helping me. Will you?"

The captain, dressed in a cut-up leather glove, stuttered for a moment, then asked, "But what can we do? When Brixton's army marches into Chelming—which may have already happened—they can step on us like mice."

"But we're smarter than mice, aren't we?" Janet said, balancing atop her mare's headstall and putting hands to hips. "How many men have you? I see there are," she counted quickly, "ten horses. We can put a lot of people on ten horses. But we need to hurry. I want to meet King Montgomery's army before it gets too far into Chelming."

The hope blossoming on Captain Patterson's face made Janet smile. "So you're with me, captain?"

"Tell me your plan," he said. "I—no, *we*," he said, gesturing at the oddly dressed little men falling into formation on the roadside, "shall do what we can to save Chelming from the foul machinations of King Montgomery."

The sorcerer Searorun rode beside King Montgomery, columns of soldiers at their backs. They crossed through the guardpost into Chelming, ready for any challenge—but none came. The fields were empty, and no one in the village of Over Lemming raised an alarm, though the army made enough noise to send a cow grazing along the fencerow lumbering off in panic.

The king called a halt, and he and Searorun leapt from their horses. They strode to the first cottage. Searorun jerked the door open, peered inside, then beckoned to the king. In the late sunlight streaming through the doorway, they could see that all within was normal—no overset tables or benches, no bloodstains—but no people, either. Only empty clothing, lying in heaps.

All through the town it was the same. Empty houses. The only movement came from the occasional cat or chicken startled from a nap.

"Have you seen enough, Sire?" Searorun asked. "Just as I promised. Every man, woman and child in Chelming is gone. The kingdom is yours."

"Over Lemming is hardly the entire kingdom," King Montgomery growled, but then he slapped Searorun on the back. The sorcerer winced and stepped back. "But you've made your point—"

A cat leaped, squalling horrifically, from a roof onto Searorun's head. "Die, foul invaders!" a tiny voice screamed. As Searorun frantically tried to grab the cat, he felt a prick on the side of his neck, and the same voice said, "Don't move, or I'll stab you." He froze.

He and King Montgomery were surrounded by perhaps a hundred people no taller than his boot top, all brandishing knives as if they were swords. The screeches of their high-pitched voices made a bewildering din. As the king tried to stomp on the tiny men, they danced out of the way. Soon they were clambering up the skirts of his riding tunic, and though he shook some off, there were too many for him. "What *is* this, Searorun?" Montgomery roared. "There should be no one, big *or* small, left in Chelming!"

The cat on Searorun's head chose this moment to leap away, leaving bleeding scratches across his face. But his torment did not cease. The voice cried in his ear, "So you *are* the sorcerer who cast this spell!" and he felt another jab in the side of his neck.

"Who are you? Why are you plaguing me?" he asked, trying not to move his face as he spoke.

"I am Janet, daughter of the Duke of Arbinclose," the voice in his ear said. The pain in his neck grew. "You did this to me—I recognize your voice. And I'm not even from Chelming."

"What?" said Searorun, forgetting to be circumspect and getting jabbed harder.

"You shrank me—and my escort. We were fully two leagues into Deccalia."

"But . . . the spell was carefully designed to make the people of *Chelming* disappear," Searorun sputtered.

"They did not disappear—only got smaller. When I rode into Chelming to find out who had shrunk me, I found the same everywhere. All, from soldiers to the smallest babe, the size of children's poppets."

Searorun crept his left hand toward the diminutive lady on his right shoulder. If he could catch her. . . .

"Hold still, or I'll shove this needle into your neck up to its eye. And I have more."

He stopped moving.

"So, will you release the spell?"

"It will require weeks of preparation." He let a whine creep into his voice. "I'll need to gather materials, and my apprentices aren't here—"

The needle jabbed his neck again. "I don't believe you. I've studied the basics of magic, and I know that no matter how complicated the spell, there will be a quick way to release it if need be. If, for example, King Montgomery didn't pay what he promised."

Searorun thought. If he shook his body suddenly, the tiny woman should fall to the ground, and he could step on her, if it so pleased him.

Action followed thought—and agony followed action. She must have had a firm hold on the collar of his robe. The needle jabbed full into his neck, and he gritted his teeth against the pain.

"Undo the spell!" Janet cried.

"I must get something from my pouch," he said between his teeth, shuddering at the feel of blood running down his neck.

"I don't trust you. You'll try something against me. Tell me what to do. And just in case you try aught else, I've another needle against the big vein in your neck."

Searorun closed his eyes and thought a spell at the creature on his shoulder. Nothing happened. Of course. Her needles were silver and negated the spell, weaker because he could not speak it aloud.

"Well?" She jabbed, and a second runnel of blood started down his neck.

"In my pouch. A glass ball."

"Lord Henry, I need you," Lady Janet called, and one of the tiny folk holding King Montgomery at bay hurried over, looking up at her. "Yes, my lady?"

"There's a glass ball in his pouch. Get it, please. Carefully."

Searorun suffered the minuscule creature to climb the folds of his robe. He briefly considered kicking out and sending the little man flying, but thought better of it when the needle jabbed at his neck once more.

Lord Henry wedged himself under Searorun's belt, released the clasp on his pouch, and removed the smoky gray ball, holding it cradled between both arms. "I have it, my lady,"

"What is it?" asked Lady Janet.

"This orb holds the souls of all the folk of Chelming," Searorun said. "I wrought great sorcery to place—"

"They seemed in full possession of their souls when I rallied them to fight King Montgomery's army," she interrupted. "How do you release the spell?"

"Break the orb."

"And how do I know that won't kill us all?"

That was what he was counting on. "We'll see." Before either small person could react, he seized the glass bubble and crushed it in his fist.

The needle jabbed deep into Searorun's neck, then a weight grew on his shoulder, and fingers closed around his throat as he sank to the ground. His oxygen-starved brain, struggling to find a spell that would release him, was further distracted by a blood-curdling scream. "It worked!"

Janet found herself standing in the dust of Over Lemming, naked as a baby and surrounded by yelling soldiers, panicked horses, squalling cats, and naked villagers. Lord Henry, hands clenched around Searorun's neck, blushed and looked away.

"I'll have that," she said calmly. She unclasped Searorun's belt and jerked his open-fronted robe off, taking advantage of how weakly his hands scrabbled at the fingers tight around his throat to pull the sleeves off his arms. After she settled it over her own body and pulled it tight with Searorun's belt, she turned to King Montgomery. The king stood fuming in the midst of a circle of men who flourished knives, pitchforks, and commandeered swords and looked very menacing in their hairy nakedness.

"I'm afraid, Your Majesty, that you've got a problem," Janet said. "The whole kingdom of Chelming is understandably annoyed with you. And I fear you've angered others who, like myself, are from Deccalia. My father, the Duke of Arbinclose, for instance."

She grinned as Montgomery blanched. "I think you and your pet sorcerer had better think quickly."

While the inhabitants of Over Lemming had surrounded the king and his sorcerer, the other Chelmingar Janet had recruited, led by Captain Patterson and his company, had subdued King Montgomery's soldiers. The tiny size of the Chelmingar had taken the army completely by surprise, and now naked farmers and millers, soldiers and seamstresses were holding the Brixtish soldiers' own weapons at their throats.

"You fool!" King Montgomery, now purple in the face, raged at Searorun. "Your spell failed utterly."

Lord Henry had released the sorcerer and disappeared—probably to find clothing. Searorun, who with his emerald-green robe gone proved to be wearing an astonishingly yellow shirt and chausses, stood massaging his bruised throat. He'd pulled her needles from his neck and dropped them into the dirt. "What kind of fool are you, trusting everything to a spell?" he retorted. "Your agents should have been all through Chelming, waiting to take over when the people disappeared. As it is, your troops were thwarted by a mob of Thumbkins!"

"I didn't notice you resisting them any better," King Montgomery began, but Janet cut in.

"You can continue your argument later," she informed them. "Right now, I think you'd better talk to my father."

The Duke of Arbinclose, middle-aged but wiry and tough, rode up on a black war horse caparisoned in silver. "What is the meaning of this, Montgomery?" he thundered. "I received a message from my daughter saying you—"

"Good evening, Father," Janet said.

"Oh, there you are, Janet," the Duke greeted her calmly. "A bit taller than I was expecting, from your message."

"The spell's broken," she said. "You probably ought to do something to keep him," she pointed at Searorun, "from trying anything else. He's the one who laid the spell."

The Duke beckoned to his men, who had followed him into the village, and before the sorcerer could finish the spell he muttered under his breath they had him tied and gagged and slung over the back of a horse.

"Now for you," the Duke told King Montgomery. "It seems the Chelmingar captured you honestly."

"There's a cart load of treasure just the other side of the border—they can have that if they set me free!" the king babbled.

"They already *have* the treasure," Janet observed.

The village headman approached the Duke, bowing deeply. "She did it all, sir. When we were fuddled by the spell, finding ourselves so small, Lady Janet rode through Chelming and gathered us up and made an army! And she just as small, and not even from here." He bowed to Janet, then dropped to his knees before her. "My lady, you have the thanks of every Chelmingar."

The villagers threatening King Montgomery muttered agreement. "So brave she were!" "She come up with it all on her own, how to fight those Brixtish soldiers." "She said even if we's small as mice, we din't have to be timid as mice!"

"Well, my dear, you've done a good job here," the Duke told Janet. She smiled and bowed to him. "Only as you have taught me, Father," she said quietly.

"Much good may come of this muddle," the Duke mused, beckoning to his men to take King Montgomery into custody.

Much good *did* come of the incident. Lady Janet of Arbinclose married Montgomery etc. etc. the Fourth, to became Queen of Brixton, as Montgomery the Third was forced to abdicate in his son's favor. She forged close ties of friendship between Brixton and both Chelming and Deccalia. King Montgomery was exiled to a small island off the coast of Deccalia, and the sorcerer Searorun was banished to Far Ensurenki—where it is rumored he blew himself and a third of the Ensurenki army into oblivion.

Queen Janet reined in her horse as a huge voice boomed, seemingly out of nowhere, "Woe, woe, people of the kingdom of Brixton. This day art thou doomed."

"Oh no you don't," Janet muttered under her breath. As the Queen's Guard surrounded her, she took a bulky packet from her belt pouch and held it high in the air, as if letting it see the surrounding countryside.

She had been afraid something like this might happen, and had worked with the most puissant sorcerers of Brixton, Chelming, and Deccalia to prepare for this eventuality.

The booming voice continued, "This day will you die most horribly. Know ye, people of Brixton, that this is the work of King Ottfried Oled Prasfalk Sigwill of Ensurenki."

"Whatever happens, say nothing," Janet told her guards. She crushed the packet between her palms, and a sharp, musty odor permeated the air around her.

"Before you die, you will know the futility of resisting King Ott—" The booming pronouncement cut off in mid-word with a strangled squawk.

She smiled. The packet seemed to have worked just as the sorcerers had said it would, sending the spell back against whoever cast it. She waited for a moment to see if anything else happened. The horses began to look for grass to eat. Finally she turned in her saddle, and said to her guards, "I believe we can go on now."

"Majesty?" the captain of her Guard asked. "Is all well?"

"Oh yes," Janet said, wrapping the packet in a piece of silk and putting it in a drawstring bag. "Just dealing with another problem neighbor."

Changes of Life

The stench of death filled Goody Sarah Albright's nostrils and the bawling of unmilked cows rang in her ears. On the pallet near the cottage's fireplace Kate stirred, but Goody Albright caught her daughter's hands and held them before the girl could scratch at her face. Wishing it would stop the pain, Goody Albright washed the wound along Kate's cheekbone yet again. Kate moaned, and Goody Albright gritted her teeth. She knew how this felt, all too well—a week ago she had moaned and thrashed while Kate had done the same to her wounds.

She closed her eyes to still rising tears. She could not lose Kate, too.

A knock on the door, then the inquiry, "Are any alive within?" She limped over to lift the bar and open the door.

Two elderly women stood without—one gaunt, with thinning gray hair pulled back in an untidy bunch, the other plump and dressed all in black. No one Goody Albright knew. Why had they come to this village of the dead?

"Are you healers?" she asked. "Don't risk yourselves; I have this well enough in hand."

Their gaze dropped to her bandaged foot, touched her scarred forearm. "We aren't healers, goody, and we don't fear the pestilence. We've come because magic created the flesh rot, and only magic can remove it," said the thin woman.

Magic. That would explain how quickly the pestilence had fallen on Lexby, and how none of the surrounding villages seemed to be afflicted. "You're wise women?" Goody Albright asked. They looked like anyone's grandmothers, threadbare and wrinkled.

The plump one answered, "Indeed."

"Now," said the thin one, "Show us your sick, and we'll remove the disease."

"It left my flesh," Goody Albright said, "and you're much too late for my man. But my daughter. . . ."

They followed her to the pallet by the fireside and knelt beside Kate. They studied the wound on her cheek. "You've been cleaning it?" the plump one asked.

"With sweetflag juice and an infusion of everlasting. They were the only remedies to slow the decay," Goody Albright said.

"Without our magic, that's true." The thin one held her hand above the wound. "The disease is nearly gone. There is another wound, though. . . ."

Goody Albright loosened the strings at her daughter's throat and drew down her blouse. "Here, on her shoulder." The flesh was black, the smell almost more than she could tolerate. It was much worse than it had been—in the center the bone showed through, pale amidst the rotting flesh. "The cleaning hasn't helped much, as you see."

"Dear God," said the plump wise woman, "may we not be too late." She held her right hand above Kate's shoulder, reached out with the left to grasp the thin woman's hand. The thin wise woman held her left hand near the plump one's right hand. They closed their eyes.

No incantations, no potions or glowing talismans—but the blackened flesh melted and pink appeared in the wound's center, then moved outward. It still gaped dangerously deep, but no longer showed any sign of the flesh rot.

They remained motionless for many heartbeats, then the thin one sighed and opened her eyes. "The disease is gone from her body. Burn that blouse, though, and any cloth that's touched the wounds." She looked pointedly at the rag Goody Albright had used to lave Kate's face.

The plump wise woman opened her eyes, face pale, and said, "This wound might still kill her. It's deep, I couldn't—"

"You did what you could," her companion interrupted. She turned to Goody Albright. "Cover the wounds with sphagnum. The scars will heal cleaner if you make a cream of irish moss and bedstraw herb and rub it into the wound."

"Yes, I have those." Goody Albright had made the washes and creams when the pestilence first came to Lexby, and Kate had treated her wounds with them. They'd tried to treat Titus, but his hands. . . . No time for that. God sent these women to heal Kate, now Sarah must do her best to keep her daughter alive.

The thin wise woman helped the other to her feet and they started for the door. "You've done well, goody," said the thin one. "Would you consider traveling with us?"

"I can't do that," said Goody Albright. *Why did they suggest such a thing?* "I must tend Kate and the farm. I have responsibilities here in Lexby. But before you leave can I make you tea? We have no bread—"

"Thank you; there's no time. We must help your neighbors."

"My thanks then, and God go with you."

Goody Albright dropped the bar into place once more and turned to Kate. The girl slept, chest rising and falling in natural breathing.

Goody Albright bent a knee for a moment in prayer. "Please, save my daughter." Then she took the jar from a kitchen shelf and dabbed cream into Kate's wound. She wondered if flesh rot struck in Hillborough or Kenham. Could any place in the kingdom be safe from a magic-borne pestilence?

A week later Kate was sitting up in Goody Albright's bed, hugging the pieced quilt around her and sipping broth while her mother rubbed cream into the broad angry mark marring her cheekbone. "Now stop worrying about finding me a husband, mother," she said. "Who will have me when I look like this?"

"Don't you say that, Kate. Why, it looks better every day." Goody Albright finished and collapsed into the chair—the one Titus had made, just after their marriage.

"Good, then you'll let me up."

"Your shoulder—"

"Mother, I can work with one hand. *You* should rest—I've seen how you limp. Your leg's bothering you, tell me true."

Kate had the right of it. Goody Albright's thigh ached where the flesh rot had eaten away skin and muscle. Neither it nor her foot, missing two toes now, were healing well. But the cows must be milked, and the chickens fed. If she didn't make bread, she and Kate wouldn't eat.

She swallowed, gulping down despair and pain. Perhaps she should let Kate help—her shoulder wound had closed up well.

Goody Albright swallowed again, her mouth dry. It was too hot in the little bedroom; how could Kate stand the quilt so close around her? "I'm getting a drink, will you be all right?"

"You fret too much, mama. I'll be fine."

When Goody Albright lay her aching body down on the pallet by the kitchen fire the sun had long set. It felt good to be still, to know the cows were fed, the chickens in their coop, all cared for, the cottage swept—if not in the best manner. Now she could sleep 'til dawn, when the cows would need her again.

Sleep would not come. What would she do at harvest time, without Titus? Titus had been a quiet man, a slow man and exacting. Goody Albright missed him lying at her side, thinking long and long before saying, "Sarah, we will sell the piglets at market Tuesday next." She would not remember how the flesh rot had taken his hands, how he had suffered in silence through all her ministrations, however painful.

Aah, now the kitchen fire had flared. She sat up and found it still banked, almost out. *Nay, I'm just too hot again.* She lay down, favoring the slowly healing thigh.

So hot, so hot. Titus. . . .

What about Kate? What man will want her with her face scarred? She cannot run the farm herself when I'm gone.

So hot.

The dawn found Goody Albright still worrying, sleepless.

"Oh, mama, I can't go anywhere." Kate covered her scarred cheek with spread fingers. "I can't let anyone see *this*."

"It is much better, love. No one in the village will notice. They've seen worse—all of them."

"Is the village really that bad?" Kate asked, pausing as she tried, one-handed, to tie her bodice-laces.

"You'll see."

Goody Albright limped along beside Kate, finding the least-rutted section of the road into the village center. On both sides untended fields showed golden. Nearly harvest time.

In the commons before the headman's house a pitiful knot of people gathered. Remnants of families stood together, staring sidelong to see how their neighbors had fared. Only three of the Beck's ten? Goodman Beck, gaunt and pale, missing fingers from both hands. *He was luckier than Titus.*

Two little Decker girls clung to Widow Marshal's skirts, and young Avery Marshal leaned on a crutch, half one leg gone. *I am luckier than he,* thought Goody Albright.

Goody Leer and Goody Yarrow stood together, heads covered with black kerchiefs; had neither of their husbands survived?

The reason they had all gathered, a middle-aged man in the king's gold and blue livery, stood on the far side of the commons. He backed off when the villagers approached him, looking from face to face, his adam's apple bobbing as his gaze moved from one deformity to the next.

"People of Lexby," began the kingsman. His voice cracked; he cleared his throat and continued, "I bring a message from your sovereign, King Thomas of Trauland." He read from a roll of creamy parchment. "The wizards of Pantaj sent flesh rot to Lexby and Norberg, Nether Thatchhold and Emmer. King Thomas's wizards struck back, and now Pantaj suffers worse than did our kingdom."

A low moan from the villagers. "How could any suffer worse than we have?" growled Old Man Gray.

The kingsman licked his lips. "The wise women have declared this village clean, free of pestilence."

"Now that most of my family is gone," muttered Goodman Beck.

"And these wee lambs' mama and papa," said Widow Marshal.

Headman Preece, one arm in a sling and his head bandaged, stepped from his cottage doorway. "Hush, listen to what the man has to say."

The kingsman mopped his brow with one sleeve and continued, "The war has taken a grievous toll on the kingdom, and King Thomas has decreed that all able-bodied men will take up arms against the Pantaj."

The muttering turned to an outraged howl. "There *are* no able bodied in Lexby," Avery Marshal said, "the Pantaj have seen to that. Go and leave us honest folk alone."

"Nevertheless, you must prepare. King Thomas has spoken." The kingsman rolled the parchment, pushed it inside his jacket, and marched from the commons.

"How can he do this to us? What about the harvest?" asked Widow Marshal. Others echoed her, complaining that they could barely survive as it was, without losing more family members.

"'Tis as young Avery said, we have no able bodied. Lexby is in sore straits now, e'en without the king's command." Headman Preece's harsh voice cut through the others. "What will we do when the armies march through?" His jaw working, he turned, strode into his cottage, and closed the door.

Old Man Gray whispered so loud all could hear, "His Mary lost an eye—and her wits, it seems, when her babe died."

Goody Albright's eyes were hot and tight, and her head ached with unshed tears. *How could I forget what the others have suffered?* she thought. *I spent all my time bemoaning my fate, and Titus's, and Kate's.*

Kate's voice shook as she said, "Let's go home, mother."

Goody Albright's back and shoulders ached from swinging the scythe, but pitifully little of the field had been harvested. Kate gathered the corn into sheaves and tied them; her shoulder had not healed enough to let her wield the scythe.

August sun beat down, and Goody Albright wiped sweat from her forehead with a grimy hand. "Though I'd not wish for rain on our harvest," she commented to Kate, "A cloud over the sun would be welcome."

"Aye," agreed Kate wearily. "Mother, how can you keep going? My shoulder's afire, and my mouth dry as Larsen's well."

"Drink, then. We can't rest long—whether we'll live through winter or no depends on how much we harvest now."

Goody Albright limped to the bucket she'd left at the field's edge and sipped tepid water from the dipper. She passed the dipper to Kate, who drank most of its contents and splashed the rest on her scarlet face. "Why don't we move to town, mother? The farm's too much for the two of us."

"Nay, Kate, we'll survive this winter, and then we'll find you a husband to run the farm."

"What man would take me, with this face?" Kate ran her fingers over the scar, as Goody Albright had seen her do a hundred times in a day.

"'Tis not as bad as—" began Goody Albright.

Kate interrupted her. "Look, mother, how very strange."

Goody Albright thought Kate was trying to change the tide of the discussion—until she turned and looked where Kate pointed, east across the wasteland. Gray clouds moved in a curtain across the sky and engulfed the sun in moments. She'd seen clouds come in that fast when a hailstorm battered the fields back in the last year of King Matthew's reign. "That's hail! There's naught we can do but get to shelter."

The two ran for the shed and huddled between nervous cows as the hail pounded past. When they ventured out into the now-cool afternoon, they expected to see the fields destroyed, the crops pulped. But though hailstones had battered the wasteland to the east, and the hedgerows along the Kenham road were leafless, the fields were untouched. Kate kicked at a pile of melting hailstones. "Have you ever seen such a thing, mother?"

"Nay, these are strange times indeed."

They returned to the harvest and Goody Albright picked up the scythe. Her fingers started to tingle, her heart pounded, and heat rose to drench her body in sweat. Breathing hard, she stopped, and Kate ran to her. "What's the matter, mother?"

"Nothing, just feeling . . . odd."

"That's happened often of late, mother." Kate cocked her head and grinned. "Mother, could be it's your change of life?"

Goody Albright stared open mouthed at her daughter. The heat faded from her face, suddenly as it had come, and she shook her head ruefully. "You could well be right, daughter. Why did I not think—but with the pestilence, and the harvest...."

Another sign of her advancing years, and Kate with no one else to care for her. The scar on Kate's face was better, wasn't it? Goody Albright looked at its fading red. Yes, the edges were smoothing. Rubbing cream in did it good.

Kate seemed to know her thoughts. "Mother, the change of life doesn't mean you'll die within the year. I'd wager you'll live longer than Old Man Gray—you're too stubborn to die, the pestilence proved that." She softened her words with a smile, and put an arm around her mother's shoulders.

"Ah, Kate, what can we do?"

"Finish the harvest; the next hailstorm may not be so obliging."

Goody Albright rose wearily from the milking stool. She released the cow from her ties and shooed her from the shed, then poured the milk into the stone cooling pan.

A scuffle of feet on the path outside. "Sarah!" Widow Marshal rushed in, breathing hard. "The Pantaj come! Delsey Decker saw them while she was out nutting and ran to tell me, bless the child. What shall we do? They'll kill us, or worse."

Worse, thought Goody Albright grimly. We're a village of women and children now the King's had our men off to the army. "Have you sent

Delsey to tell our neighbors?"

"I have. Where can we hide? We've nowhere to go, nothing—"

"Send your Avery and the girls off into the woods with your livestock. Avery can't help us, with his crippled leg. Bring anything you can find for a weapon. We're all Lexby has, now."

"You're right, Sarah." Widow Marshal hurried back down the path, hiking her skirts so she could move faster.

Kate was in the house making bread; something she could do one-handed. "Drive the cattle into the forest," Goody Albright ordered, her gaze sweeping across her tidy kitchen to find a weapon. "Avery Marshal and the little Decker girls should already be there. The Pantaj come."

"Nay, mother, I'll stay with you." Kate wiped her hands on her apron and dropped it on the hearth. "Don't send me off with the children."

"Your arm. . . ."

Kate clumsily tied her hair under a kerchief and picked up a poker. "I'll need but one hand to wield this."

"Very well, then." For an instant, panic stabbed through Goody Albright's gut. It was easy to risk her own life, but Kate. . . . A tiny voice wailed inside her, *I'll lose everything—my daughter, my home, my farm.* She stopped on the doorstep, closed the cottage's heavy wooden door, and clenched her fists. She would not give way to weakness now.

A straggle of goodwives, half-grown boys and Old Man Gray stood in the Kenham road, white-faced and flustered. "They come—I hear them!" cried young Jonathan Preece. Though the pitchfork trembled in his grasp, he stepped to the forefront.

The rest formed up behind him; they heard it too, a tramp of feet, calls in strange accents.

Something rose in Goody Albright as she stood, scythe in hand, between Widow Marshal and Kate. More than the heat of her change of life, much more. This army marching toward Lexby—they had killed Titus in agony. They had maimed her and Kate, caused death and suffering throughout Lexby. Now they marched to finish what the pestilence had begun.

Someone behind her muttered prayers, but hatred burned through Goody Albright. God forgive her, she felt naught but hate for the Pantaj army.

"If only the pestilence were still alive in Lexby, and the Pantaj might feel it in *their* flesh as we did in ours." She had not meant to say that aloud, and the savage words of assent from the villagers crowded around her sent a shiver of horror down her back. What have we all become?

Then the first Pantaj came into view, armored and carrying spears, smelling of dust and sweat and some strange pungent spice. The column stopped when they saw the villagers gathered in the road; soldiers laughed and whistled.

Goody Albright knew then that the villagers' efforts would be vain. She hoped the children and the crippled would get to the forest. She and her companions would slow the Pantaj for mere moments, but she would face them and fight. Such was her nature.

She stepped forward and raised her scythe. Beside her, Kate did the same, and Widow Marshal. The entire little army of Lexby surged toward their foe.

The foremost soldier, a scar-faced man with a chin-long moustache, lost his grin. His eyes widened. "Plague!" he screamed. "The plague is here." His spear, which had been aimed at Goody Albright's chest, wavered.

She raced forward, swung her scythe, and felt a satisfying crunch as the spear's shaft shattered. The soldier backed into his fellows, hands raised before his face. Villagers attacked the army with brooms and rakes and hoes, and the soldiers fell back before them.

The smell of death swirled through the struggle; the flesh rot's gut-wrenchingly familiar odor. Goody Albright raised her scythe again, then stepped aside as Kate jostled her elbow, and looked her daughter in the face.

The scar on Kate's cheek gaped black-edged and raw, the dull ivory of her jawbone showing through. Goody Albright almost lost her grip on the scythe when she saw the blackened, stinking flesh on her own forearm. What foul magic had brought back the pestilence, to kill them surely as the soldiers' spears?

As awareness of the flesh rot's return struck the villagers they faltered; then they raised their improvised weapons and charged into the Pantaj ranks. As they died of the plague, their enemy would die with them.

Goody Albright struck at the backs of fleeing Pantaj with her scythe, running after them fast as her hindering skirts and bad leg would let her. When she lurched to a stop, sobbing for breath, the Pantaj had disappeared—all but those who lay still on the Kenham road.

Slowly the villagers of Lexby gathered, panting and dragging farm tools and a few captured spears. Kate came back last, haggard and pale. The scar on her face looked just as it had before—red and ridged, but with no trace of flesh rot.

The silent group stared at Goody Albright. "It wasn't real," said Widow Marshal. "But we saw—we *smelled*—the pestilence."

"'Twas God's hand," said Goody Leer. "He answered your prayer, Sarah, in His own way."

Goody Albright hoped it had indeed been God's hand, not the

hatred twisting in her heart, but she said nothing.

Young Jonathan Preece, eyes bright with victory, asked, "Will the Pantaj come back? Liza took Mam into the woods. Should I go find them, and take them home?"

"Nay, lad, find your mother and make her comfortable 'neath a tree," said Old Man Gray, who'd fought in his younger days. "E'en the pestilence won't keep the enemy from Lexby for long."

"By heaven, mother, look at this," called Kate from the milking shed. Goody Albright tied the last of her keepsakes into a cloth and went out to see what put the hysterical edge into her daughter's voice.

The milk in the cooling pan, fresh that morning, had curdled into yellow, stinking lumps.

"Hail that misses the crops, an illusion of pestilence, and now the milk spoiled," cried Kate. "Strange magic lies on Lexby."

Goody Albright's fingers tingled and she shuddered. "Strange magic," she said, realization boiling into her mind. "Always when I'm about. When I wanted clouds to block the sun I got them—but hail came too. *I* wished the Pantaj ill, and got a seeming of pestilence."

"Do you think. . . ?"

"Could it be my change of life does more than take away fertility? 'Tis said a wise woman gains her power then." Goody Albright raised her hands and stared at them, as if they belonged to someone else.

Kate gestured at the spoiled milk. "You think *you* did this, all unaware?"

"If I have, 'twill be no help to us now, for I cannot control it." She strode from the milking shed, back to the house. "Come, let us take to the woods ere the army returns."

Goody Albright tied bread and cheese into another cloth, gathered her bundle of treasures, and called to Kate. "Have you rounded up the cows?"

"By heaven, mother, it's too late." Kate ran into the house and barred the door. "The Pantaj are back!"

Late afternoon sunlight glanced off spearheads and helmets of the Pantaj army, almost at the edge of the Albright fields. Goody Albright closed the window shutters and leaned against them. "Kate, my love, will you forgive me?"

"'Tis not your fault, mother. We should have left our things and fled with the others."

Sounds—the Pantaj shouting orders, then running feet. The two peered through the crack between the shutters, and saw bowmen spreading out all along the Kenham road. The archers knelt and companions handed them knobby-headed arrows. One by one, the archers loosed.

"Those are fire arrows. They'll burn the village."

Goody Albright shuddered. She looked around her cottage, still tidy despite their hasty packing. She thought of the chickens, muttering and clucking in their coop, and the cows in the field. All the things she and Titus had gathered and raised and loved together. Most of all Kate, her youngest daughter, the one she'd always loved most—though she'd never tell. Now they'd all be gone, burned and blackened, to be buried like Titus 'neath the fertile Lexby soil.

"If I have magic, let it work for me now!" she cried. "Make the arrows miss, make the archers stumble."

No magic spoiled the archers' aim; another volley of fire arrows landed in thatch and dry fields. One, two, a dozen wisps of smoke rose throughout Lexby's fields and cottages.

"Oh, if only they did not know the village was here," said Goody Albright. Her skin started to itch. "Where is the king's army, which has done naught for Lexby but rob us of our menfolk?" Her fingers tingled and a buzzing, like Widow Marshal's bees, rose in her head.

"Mother, look!" The archers wavered, not loosing their arrows. Some stood and shaded their eyes, squinting at Lexby's cottages. An order rang out and they loosed, but none of the arrows found their way into the thatched roofs.

"You *do* have magic!" Kate seized Goody Albright and pulled her into a hug, her smile and the shine in her eyes enough to make her beautiful again, despite the scar. "What shall we call you now—Wise Woman Sarah?"

"Don't rejoice yet," cautioned Goody Albright, trying to scratch between her shoulder blades. "There are more, many more. It would take the king's army, jumping out of hiding from behind the barns and byres, to chase them away, I fear."

"Can you make us look like something else, think you, so we can escape to the woods?" asked Kate.

Goody Albright had forgotten their own plight. They would be burned in their cottage—or worse, if the soldiers found them first. "I don't know how the magic works."

"Just say it—say what you want, mother. Make us look like wheat sheaves. They'd probably kill a cow."

They did not need to hide, for out from behind cottages and sheds came ghostly soldiers—warriors from children's tales, with flashing swords and gleaming armor. Goody Albright grew almost frantic with itching, but stayed by the crack in the window shutters to watch the illusory warriors chase the Pantaj back toward the border. Then she took a bucket to help put out the fire in her neighbor's thatch.

"You can't stay, mother. You don't know what your magic will do." A week later Kate and Goody Albright—or Wise Woman Sarah, as the villagers had already begun calling her—argued as they scrubbed the cottage's wooden floor. "All the cows dried up when you sent the ghost soldiers after the Pantaj. The village can't survive more such reactions."

"I want to stay here—this is my home." Sarah set the brush on the hearth, wiped her hands on her apron, and pushed herself to her feet with a grunt. "I have no wish to roam Trauland's roads, a lone woman, 'til I find a wise woman to teach me."

"I'll be with you, mother!"

"That you won't! If I go you must stay and tend the farm."

"I can't care for the farm by myself. The two of us together can scarce finish all the tasks."

"Widow Marshal says her Avery will aid you as he can, and the oldest Dexter girl can help with the household tasks." Sarah drew the bread from the little brick oven and closed her eyes to better enjoy the heady aroma.

Kate stood, put fists to hips and faced her mother. "If I promise to stay will you go? If I keep your precious house and farm, will you get the training you need to keep Lexby safe *from* your magic?"

Sarah glared at her daughter; then laughter spilled over. "We are too much of a kind, my love. Aye, I'll go—but mind you well, I'll come back. Lexby is my home. *I* have no wish to go."

"I have little wish to stay, so we both go against our wills to do the best."

Sarah gathered a bundle of clothing, and while Kate prepared bread and cheese and dried meat for the road Sarah walked the paths between the cottages and said her goodbyes to the villagers. Then she gave Kate one last hug. "I will come back to stay," she said, and took up her bundles.

"If you do not outgrow Lexby. Goodbye, mother." Kate shooed her out the door and closed it.

When Sarah reached the Kenham road she turned to look at her snug cottage. It had not been so when she married Titus; together they had built it up. How hard it was to leave. She sighed, adjusted her bundle, and limped toward Kenham, leaning on the cane Avery Marshal had made for her. *Perchance I'll learn a spell to make my Kate whole again.*

A woman standing at the Avesburgh crossroads looked up and smiled at her. With a catch in her heart, Sarah recognized the plump wise woman, the one who'd taken the pestilence off Kate. "Where are you headed, Sarah?" the woman asked. "Will you travel with me now?"

"It seems I must," said Sarah, and fell into step beside the other wise woman.

Strength, Wisdom, and Compassion

Scented steam rose from the enameled tub in the bathhouse behind the witch Hyacinth's cottage. "Renata," Hyacinth said as Queen Renata disrobed, neatly folding her clothing on a bench, "I beg of you. Reconsider now, before it's too late."

The queen turned a serene face to the witch. "Hyacinth, I've made my decision. Everyone in Orthefell suffered when Terzo killed my husband and declared himself king. When he decided to seal that kingship by marrying me, this became necessary."

Hyacinth lowered her voice. "This is likely to be more dangerous to the child growing within you than to you, at this stage. This child is all you have left of Bhaltair."

"Both he and I will need strength to survive under Terzo's rule," Renata said, voice rough. She stepped onto the stool beside the tub and let herself down into the orange-tinged water. It rose along her body as she slid down, until she sat nearly neck deep. She ran her fingers through her long chestnut hair, unraveling its braids, letting it float on the water's surface.

Hyacinth, a plain woman who looked no more than twenty years old but was much older, sighed. It was done, and she could not call back her actions now. The queen had chosen her path.

Renata took a deep breath and slid completely beneath the water, hair slowly sinking to stick in thick clumps on her shoulders. After a long time she surfaced. Water droplets, now bereft of color and scent, ran down her pale face.

"Is it done?" she asked.

"Yes, Your Majesty," Hyacinth said.

"Don't call me 'Your Majesty'. You were my nurse long before I was Bhaltair's wife. Long before Terzo coveted our kingdom. To you, I will always be simply Renata."

Hyacinth sighed again. She shouldn't make a habit of that; people didn't like their witch sounding like a lovesick girl. "Yes, Renata. You can come out now." She steadied the queen as she stepped out of the tub, then handed her a towel so she could dry herself.

Once the queen's body was dry, Hyacinth wrapped her still-damp hair in the towel and helped her into her shift. Renata stood barefoot on the bathhouse's warm tiles while Hyacinth combed her hair and braided it expertly into all its tiny plaits, then coiled it atop Renata's head. She helped the queen into her bridal splendor—gown of gold silk and pearls, overgown of cream silk and diamonds, robe of midnight blue adorned with cream lace at throat and cuffs. Last of all, Hyacinth pinned the crown into the coil of braids so that it would not slip.

Silently, Hyacinth held the queen's train as she took the stone-paved path to the road where her carriage, her armed escort, and her attendants waited. Before Renata ascended into the carriage, Hyacinth kissed her on the cheek. "Be well, love," she said, and turned away quickly, hurrying into her house. She didn't want Renata to see the tears brimming in her eyes.

Hyacinth stayed in her cottage the rest of the day, mixing spells and ignoring the sounds of celebration—trumpets, drums, muskets firing into the air. Her little Renata, who had been so happy with King Bhaltair, was now married to the usurper Terzo.

Hyacinth didn't see Renata again for a month. People came to her for spells—a woman who wanted beauty, a man who craved virility, the merchant who wished for luck, the poet who desired a muse. She explained the price of each spell—both in coin and in the spell's toll on each of them. "Is not your own native talent enough?" she asked the poet. "No one can know what toll the spell will take on you. What if you lose your eyesight in payment? Or perhaps the use of your hands?"

"I'll take the risk," he answered. "When I compose poems that bewitch the ladies, that make the nobles weep and shower gold on me—what will it matter? For then I will be wealthy, and can hire a scribe to write out the gems I speak."

Thus it had been throughout Hyacinth's life. Each person who wanted a spell was determined. What matter the future? They were concerned only with the now. So, because she was a witch, and that was her talent and destiny, she mixed the ingredients, heated the water, and prepared the bath.

The merchant took his spell packet home, to use in his own bath, but those who didn't want it known they'd purchased a spell, or had no bath at home, used Hyacinth's bathhouse. She only knew what toll the spell had taken when her eyesight became sharper, her hair more luxurious, or her face in the mirror younger.

Queen Renata summoned Hyacinth to the palace on the first day of the Month of Blooming. The witch dressed in her best, and set out on the long walk to the palace.

The changes that had taken place in the city since last she had walked this way disturbed Hyacinth. Once-prosperous shops had closed, armed and uniformed men stood on nearly every corner, and citizens walked quickly, peering nervously over their shoulders.

When she arrived at the palace and was escorted by four well-armed men to the queen's rooms, she felt shabby and out of place. Renata was surrounded by beautiful women in gowns of lace and jewels, who gossiped with high fluting voices and chirped their artificial laughter. It had not been so when Renata had been married to Bhaltair. She had worn simple wool except for state occasions, and ridden through the city on her own horse, and when she laughed, it had been a hearty guffaw. She had surrounded herself with capable and intelligent companions.

"Wise Woman Hyacinth," Renata said, and the witch was glad to hear that the Queen's voice had not suddenly shot up an octave. "I am with child. In eight months, I will require someone to care for the new prince or princess, and I thought naturally of my old nurse."

Hyacinth took a deep breath. So the child had survived the spell bath, and Renata had let the doctors examine her and discover her pregnancy. "Surely, Your Majesty, there are more suitable nurses," her gaze traveled over the twittering beauties surrounding the queen, "than I."

"None of my ladies has children of her own," Renata said. She met Hyacinth's gaze and wrinkled her nose. The witch knew they had chosen to remain childless for the sake of beauty spells. "They know nothing of child care. But you raised me. None would wish to deprive me of your expertise."

"In that case, Your Majesty, I accept, and thank you for your regard."

"I will have rooms prepared for you as I lay out the nursery. When they are complete, I'm sure you'd like to go over them, to see they are to your satisfaction. I'll send for you then." Briskly, Renata waved the lace fan she held.

Hyacinth wished she could talk to Renata without her twittering retinue. The queen had always been energetic. She had excelled at riding and hunting, and spent much of every day out of doors. But now, she had a restless energy that seemed too great for the room she occupied. Others might think it her joy in her pregnancy that put the bloom in her cheeks. Hyacinth knew better. The spell bath she had taken on the day of her marriage had not been for beauty, as her husband-to-be had been told, but for strength. If only she could know what its toll had been on the queen—and on the child she carried.

"Thank you, Your Majesty." Hyacinth curtsied and kissed the Queen's hand. As she stood, she realized Renata had slipped a scrap of paper into her hand. She didn't acknowledge it, merely left the room with her armed escort.

Hyacinth waited until she was in her own snug cottage to look at the note Renata had given her. "Wisdom! She wants a spell for wisdom!" Her cat, Pot Pie, raised his head from where he'd been napping in the sunshine warming her work table, thinking she was talking to him. "She knows as well as I do that the great abstracts are the hardest spells. Wisdom!"

She slumped into one of the sturdy wooden chairs and put her head in her arms on the table. "Wisdom," she said, through the tears that soaked into the sleeves of her best gown. "Oh, Renata."

A long time later, Hyacinth got up, shooed Pot Pie off her table, and began pulling books from the shelves, looking for the spell she needed. She had never prepared the spell for wisdom, and didn't know anyone else who had, either. She was certain there was one, but she was also certain the cost was immense. Could she substitute another spell—common sense, for instance? Of a certainty, a ruler could use common sense.

She found the spell in the old grimoire she'd inherited from the witch who had raised her. Poppy had written it in red ink—a sure sign that it was difficult and dangerous. Hyacinth copied it out. She didn't know how long it would take Renata to have rooms prepared for her in the palace, but she must start this spell now if she wished to have it complete by the time Renata called for her.

A month later, Hyacinth shooed Pot Pie away from the table where she was grinding more ingredients for the wisdom spell in her marble mortar. A vase nearby held fresh cut iris and lilies; she breathed their heady scent, but it didn't make her feel any better. She was grateful she was preparing this spell in spring, when the flowers were in bloom. Fresh flowers were so much more potent than dried ones.

She had been gathering ingredients, and brewing different parts of the spell bath, ever since the day Renata had requested it. The spell was nearly complete, and none too soon. Hyacinth had been summoned to the palace two days hence.

The flasks and tubing were purified and ready for use. She dropped flower petals and minced aloe leaves into a jar of pure almond oil, and heated them together over a flame. To the pale-green oil that dripped from the tubing she added exact amounts of four different powders—those which she had been preparing for a month—and heated it again. As the contents of the flask turned a glorious clear purple, Hyacinth removed it from the flame and carried it to the cool room.

When Hyacinth returned to the palace, she had the spell in her pocket in a bottle carved of alabaster. She hoped there would be some way to slip the bottle to Renata without anyone seeing it. Terzo would certainly not let his new wife take a spell bath while she was pregnant. Spell baths were more casually used in Vezienn, his homeland, so Hyacinth was sure Terzo knew the basics about spells and their effects. A spell bath taken by a pregnant woman endowed both mother and child with the desired quality; but both mother and child paid for the spell—and in different ways. Everyone had heard tales of deformed monsters born to women who had taken spell baths during pregnancy.

Renata had already used the spell for strength. There had been a good chance at the time that the spell would kill the barely formed child. But both mother and child were strong and healthy. Hyacinth wondered, for the thousandth time, what toll the spell had taken on them both.

As Hyacinth walked beside Renata, going through the rooms that would be hers in the palace, she glanced sideways often. Renata's restless energy enhanced her natural beauty. That must please Terzo. More's the pity. Renata did stumble often, and once she ran into a doorjamb. It was rather too early in her pregnancy for it to affect her balance. Was Renata's clumsiness caused by the spell bath?

Renata opened the door to a small room, and as they passed through Hyacinth slipped the bottle into her hand, out of sight of the bored ladies following them. "You'll have to get rid of your companions somehow," she whispered to the queen. "This is a rather obvious purple, and has a strong—though very pleasant—odor. Anyone would guess what it is."

Renata nodded. "I'll do it if I have to get up in the darkest hour of the night and bathe in a bucket. Terzo will never know. He's too busy bedding those twittering beauties."

Hyacinth squeezed her hand. "Do take care. I still can't agree with what you're doing—"

"You live in this kingdom," came Renata's furious whisper. "Do you want Terzo and his offspring to rule you? My child must be strong enough to face whatever comes, and make a fine ruler in his own right. With strength and wisdom. . . ."

"I understand." Hyacinth's whisper was almost inaudible. She didn't remind Renata that there would be payment for the bath. The queen was fully aware of that.

Though she ached to know if Renata had been able to use the spell bath—and what its consequences had been—Hyacinth was not summoned to the palace again until two months before the queen's child was due. She—and Renata—knew that the child would be 'early,' but they hoped no one else suspected.

The palace was very different now than it had been during Bhaltair's rule. New tapestries on the walls, expensive carpet underfoot, and gaudy statuary and bric-a-brac cluttering the hall were probably the least of the changes.

Hyacinth was taken to the room where she had met Renata before. The queen paced awkwardly back and forth, surrounded by chattering ladies and their useless needlework. Hyacinth looked closely at the queen, trying to discover what price she had paid for wisdom. But she seemed well enough, though restless and clumsy. The child would be a large one, that was obvious.

When Hyacinth accompanied Renata to the nursery for a final check that all was well, the ladies didn't even bother to follow. What mischief could a woman who could hardly waddle get into?

"One more spell—and it must be soon," Renata told Hyacinth. "Compassion. No matter what happens to me—or you—a king with compassion *can't* be as greedy and selfish as Terzo is.

"But is this wise? The cost—"

"It doesn't matter to me what payment the spell exacts. The child is healthy and strong. He's big enough now that I could bear him today and he would thrive, so the midwife assures me."

Hyacinth closed her eyes, praying for strength. "We may not have time," she said. "I don't have that one prepared, and it takes weeks. And how will I get it to you?" Compassion was another difficult spell—although not nearly as complex as that for wisdom. Hyacinth had never made it, because few people wanted it. Why risk the inevitable loss of some other faculty to gain compassion?

"Start moving your belongings into your rooms here at the palace. You needn't come yet, but if you leave the spell somewhere, hidden but clearly labeled. . . ."

"The coffer you gave me when you were a child—the one with my initial on the lid," Hyacinth said. Ten-year-old Renata had carved the ornate 'H' into the wood herself. She would know it.

Renata gave a half smile. "Good." They passed back into the parlor, Hyacinth half supporting the queen, who was clumsier than ever. Renata said, as if continuing a conversation they had been having, "Then you will start sending your possessions to the palace in a week? The midwife says the child is so active it may come sooner than expected."

"Yes, Your Majesty."

"I'll send a cart, and porters."

"Thank you, Your Majesty."

The reality of her move to the palace was made all the clearer when she sent off a cartload of her books and clothing. Her friend Tamarisk would live in the cottage until the young prince—or princess—no longer needed a nurse and she could return to her private life. She was apprehensive about living in such close proximity to the new King Terzo. If he came to the nursery to visit 'his' child, she would be meek and as invisible as possible. To his sort, servants were usually invisible. Perhaps he would not remember that she was a witch.

On a cold and blustery day in the Month of Storms, a carriage came from the palace. The imposing individual who stepped down from it to tell her that the Queen requested her presence had to wait. Hyacinth fed Pot Pie and gave him a last hug, gathered a bundle of things she wanted to take, left a note for Tamarisk, and closed the door. She looked back on her cottage regretfully. She would miss it, miss the independence and ability to speak her mind. But Renata was giving up so much more, living with Terzo; Hyacinth could spare a few years of a long life to raise up the next ruler of Orthefell.

Armed men were everywhere in the streets now, and few people braved the cold and possibility of tangling with the king's troops. Hyacinth missed the laughter of children playing in the snow.

As the carriage drove through the palace's main gate, a maid scurried out to tell Hyacinth that Renata was calling for her. Hyacinth left her bundle in the carriage—either it would be taken to her rooms or not, she didn't care at this point—and hurried up the stairs to the Queen's rooms.

The lying in was attended only by women, as tradition demanded, and Renata had banned her twittering companions. The only people in the room were two stolid middle-aged maids and the midwife.

Renata sat, propped up with pillows, in bed. Though she was breathing quickly, she was far too still for Hyacinth's peace of mind. Where was the restless energy that had filled the queen the last time Hyacinth had seen her?

Renata looked up as Hyacinth entered, but did not smile at her until the witch was nearly at her bed. The way Renata squinted at her made Hyacinth wonder if clarity of eyesight had been the payment for one of the spells. "I'm—so glad—you're here," she panted. "He's coming early, my baby, and I wanted—you to be here."

Now that Hyacinth could see the queen with her hair down in two plaits instead of up under a veil—as it had been the last two times she'd seen her—she thought she knew what another of the payments had been. Silver glints showed among the chestnut hairs at the crown of her head. How many years had Renata lost? More than ever, it pained Hyacinth that her gain was made at the cost of the people she helped.

"Thank you for calling me, Your Majesty," she said.

"I knew—you would want—to be here. Oh!"

The midwife and maids lifted Renata onto the birthing stool. Hyacinth, though she had birthed babies before, wasn't needed. She watched, uneasy. Why had Renata been in bed? Why not walking to ease the pain of the contractions?

The birth progressed quickly after that. When the baby was delivered, and the midwife had tied off the cord, the maids gently washed

Renata, then carried her back to the bed and covered her up. She didn't seem to notice; all her attention was for the child the midwife held.

"My child," she whispered.

"Your son," the midwife said. "Strong, for all he's early. I think he'll have your hair, Your Majesty." Indeed, the round head was covered with chestnut fuzz. With luck, Terzo would never suspect the child's true father.

As the midwife washed and swaddled the boy, Hyacinth studied him closely. She could see no deformities—he waved his arms and legs vigorously, and blinked big dark eyes when the midwife moved him closer to the lantern. What price had he paid for his mother's spell baths? There was a patch of dark skin on one shoulder, but many babies had birthmarks similar to that.

"Show him to Terzo," Renata whispered. "Show him his son."

The woman left, carrying the baby, and the maids followed her. Renata closed her eyes and went limp against Hyacinth. "It was worth it."

"What is it, Renata? What's wrong?"

"The last bath. Ever since I took it, I've been losing the use of my legs. By this morning, I couldn't stand. By the time the contractions started, not even my toes would move. But my son—he's strong, he's healthy."

Hyacinth swallowed, tears rising in her eyes.

"I've given him everything I could. He'll be the ruler Bhaltair didn't have the chance to be. He'll have strength, wisdom, and compassion."

"We still have to raise him, to teach him. Keep him from Terzo's example."

Renata sank back against the pillows and closed her eyes. "Thank all the gods I'll have you with me. You've given me the strength and wisdom to raise him the way Bhaltair would have wanted."

In a nearby room, the King of Orthefell exulted over the birth of his son. He did not ask about the child's mother.

Hyacinth had never made a bane bath in her life. She wondered grimly if, during her time here as the new prince's nurse, she would find a need to. She would be meek, she would be obedient—but if Terzo stepped outside the bounds, he would be sorry he had offended the witch who loved the queen.

Skin and Bones

Alathea and her brothers fought with *Waverunner*'s sails as storm winds drove their fishing boat closer and closer to the Long Wall. "Belay that line!" yelled Frederick over the wind's turmoil. Alathea glanced up at the rough basalt cliffs looming over the little boat and struggled with the water-soaked line.

"Get moving, Alathea," Nikolas, her oldest brother, called as she finished. "Help Frederick reef the sail."

She struggled across the swaying deck and seized the sail end as it flapped in the gale. "Nikolas, the tide's ebbing," she said. "We've got to get back out to sea before Macsen's Whirlpool sucks *Waverunner* down."

"If we're smashed to kindling on the Long Wall, the whirlpool won't make no matter," growled Nikolas. "Get that sail down."

A powerful gust tore the sail from Frederick's grip, and it whipped around and caught Alathea in the stomach. She lost her footing on the slippery deck and fell against the rail. Though she clutched at the sail for purchase, the rough canvas tore from her grasp. The boat's pitching hurled her overboard.

As the dark water closed over her head, she struck out with arms and legs, struggling to the surface. The breath she drew in was half salt spray; she coughed and retched, batting at the waves ineffectively. Even her cork belt couldn't keep her afloat in these waves. *Mother will be so angry with me.* She couldn't see *Waverunner*, and when she tried to draw a breath to shout she got more water than air. A wave broke over her head, and she spun into the cold darkness of the whirlpool. Almost calmly, as she struggled to find the surface, she thought, *It won't matter what mother thinks, if I'm drowned.*

Alathea wouldn't let the sea win. One thrashing arm found air and she pushed her head out, drew in a breath, and was dashed beneath the waves again. She tried to keep her head above water in the rushing chaos of the whirlpool, swimming until her arms and legs ached and her throat was raw from the salt.

Again the rushing, churning water sucked her under. There was no surface, and the swirling waves dragged her past rough stone. Up and down were all the same and she wondered if this was her death. She knew she could hold her breath for a long time, but this was not the same as diving off the pier. There was no bright circle of surface overhead.

Then the waves calmed, and her head broke water. She gulped in air and blinked her eyes to clear out the salt. It was dark as the hold with the hatch down; clouds must cover the moon and stars. Thanking Nemarun, God of Fish, Alathea swam toward where she heard waves break against the shore. She pulled herself from the water, shivering with cold, and collapsed.

She woke to the sound of lapping waves, footsteps, and oddly accented voices. "I seen it first, I did. If I'd said nothin', you'd never have known it were there."

"You can't get it yourself, it looks that heavy. I gets my share for helping."

It was very dark. Even with her eyes wide open, she saw no glimmer of stars or moon. Still cloudy, then, though the air was cold and still. Gods, but her legs hurt. And her arms, and her chest.

"A share then, but not half. I seen it first."

That's not Nikolas or Frederick, she thought. *Did* Waverunner *make it through the storm?* She lay on a cold, hard surface—stone, probably. The jabber of the two strangers hurt her head.

"You'll not get it wi'out my help. I deserves half."

She reached out, searching the darkness in hopes of finding something to cover her shivering body.

"Hey then, did it move?" Two sets of padding footfalls, then a sense of presence and an overpowering odor of mildew and fish. She couldn't see anything; the dark was complete. *They're talking about me!*

"Hai, it's alive," the voice said dispassionately.

"I thought it was too broken to live."

Broken? Me? She took inventory. Scrapes everywhere, but nothing broken. "I'm all right." The words croaked out through a throat scratchy with salt water. "But I'm sure cold."

Silence, then, "Well, merfolk it ain't." A moist, clammy hand touched her throat, found her pulse. "It talks," said the voice of the first arguer. "But it don't look like one of us, neither."

It's tar-dark out tonight. How can they even see me? The dark didn't bother her, but this cold place, these unnatural people, did. Where was she? Where were Nikolas and Frederick? "Please help me."

"Bring it along. If it lives, you gots a new Finder. If it dies, the boat gets patched."

The hand left her throat, grabbed her arm, and jerked her to her feet. That was too much for her woozy head, and as her knees buckled she heard First Arguer say, "Good. Need the boat fixed more'n a new Finder."

She was hoisted over a bony shoulder and carried to where she no longer heard waves on the shore; instead, water dripped. *What is he going to do with me?* The man dumped her onto a hard stone surface. "Ouch!" she said.

"Still alive, eh?" Fishy breath in her face. "Maybe you're not too bad broke after all. Can you handle a boat?"

"I can." Her mother had taught her to do everything on a fishing boat. She hated it, but she was good at it. But why should this man want to know?

"We go out next Tide Turn then." Fish-breath turned away.

"Wait!" said Alathea. This man was coarse and rough, but she didn't want to be left alone in the dark. "Um, what's your name? Do you have a blanket I can use? And . . . can I have a drink—and a light? Will you get word to my brothers that I've been found?"

"Full of questions, Sea Find? I be Hetch, and I give you nothing 'til you earn it."

"I'll freeze, Hetch." *What kind of person is Hetch? A pirate? A beach scavenger who kills anybody who gets between him and his loot?*

There was a sound of scraping, then footsteps approached her again. "Use this for now, and here's a drink. *Water*'s cheap."

She reached toward the sound of his voice, encountered the scratchy folds of a blanket, and pulled it gratefully around herself. Then she groped for the promised water.

Cold damp hands grabbed her wrist, set a wooden mug in her hand. "Can't see it? *Thought* you was a Blind. How you going to be a Finder if you can't see? I may get my boat patched yet!"

Blind? I'm not blind. I've always had the sharpest eyes in the family. Panic rose in Alathea's chest. Had something happened to her eyes?

"You sunlight people—I dunno how your eyes work. There be enough light in Folks' bodies and warm rock for me. You want a light, eh? Maybe. Maybe. Come Tide Turn I'll be back for you—give you somethin' to do." Footfalls shuffled off, leaving Alathea alone with her fear in the cold, echoing dark.

What did that mean? Light in peoples' bodies? *Could* Hetch see in this dark?

Echoing, cold, water dripping. As in a cave! Alathea drank the water as she peered into the dark, strained to see until her head pounded—with no result. She clutched the fish-smelling blanket around her, reached out to touch the uneven stone floor, traced along a rough wall to a close, jagged ceiling. A cave, then. *I'm not blind. But where am I?* She huddled down in her blanket and cried herself to sleep.

After a long time, Hetch came to get Alathea. He pushed her along until the sound of rushing water echoed through her head. "Step in now; don't overset the boat." She reached out, felt hide stretched over a framework; a round leather boat like the coracle she'd paddled as a child.

Alathea didn't need to see to paddle against the tide while Hetch fished slimy, dripping things—mostly driftwood, it felt like—from the ocean inside a cavern that echoed huge. "Where do your Finds come from?" she asked Hetch.

"Sucked in from Somewhere Else at Tide Turn, just like you. Where'd you come from? Comes up through the Pipes—goes down again, when next the Tide Turns. Ha!" Hetch leaned way out, pulled something in, and slapped it down beside Alathea. The little boat rocked, and her stomach protested. She was starving, but Hetch wouldn't feed her until she'd worked for him. At least the paddling kept her warm.

Wait, what did he just say? thought Alathea. *Comes up through the Pipes—like I did—then goes back down?* Maybe she could get away from this man and back to her family.

Since Alathea was paddling the boat, she knew when the tide turned. *Ha! It's ebbing. I'll wait—*

But Hetch had other ideas. "It's Tide Turn, Sea Find. Now we leave, before *we* go down the Pipes."

Now. Alathea stopped paddling long enough to feel the direction of the tide's retreat. Then she stood, rocking the boat alarmingly, and dove into the dark water.

The cold almost drove the breath from her lungs, but she ignored it, and swam underwater until she had to come up for a breath. Hetch was swearing, his voice almost lost in the noise of the waves. She gasped, ducked under water again, and let the great whirlpool that was forming pull her down.

This could kill me! But she had made it through before, and survived then. It hadn't been *too* long a way underwater, but she'd had the cork belt then to help buoy her. It had disappeared somewhere during her wild swim.

The next few minutes were a confusion of swirling water. It dragged her past a stone wall and scraped skin off her shoulder. There seemed to be no end to the water, to the cavern. She needed to breathe but was totally disoriented.

Finally her head broke through the water's surface. Air! She gulped it gratefully, dog paddling to keep her head out of the rushing water. But once she had stopped gasping, she realized that the space she had come to was black as the fish-god Nemarun's innards, and echoed. Just another cavern.

She dove, let the rushing water claim her body again. This time it slammed her against a rocky wall. She struggled upward, and sobbed with gratitude when her hands broke the surface. She gasped in air, shivering. She could hardly feel her hands and feet, and she was tiring rapidly. Another cavern—was there a place to rest?

She found a ledge—just a wrinkle in the rock, really—and wedged herself into it. There was no warmth in the soaked tatters of clothing she still wore, so she drew her knees close to her chest and wrapped her arms around them. Not much warmer—she was still shivering—but she could rest here a moment and then go on.

Some time later she roused herself to movement. Oh, how she dreaded going back into the water. But this time should do it—she'd be back out in daylight, sunshine to dry her, to warm her. She took a deep breath and dropped into the rushing sea. It dragged her down, scraped her past rock, and then stilled. She struggled to the surface, her energy almost gone. Tar darkness. Sobbing, she swam to the stone shore, pulled herself out, and slept.

"It *is* the same one, I say, and it's *mine*." A familiar voice, a familiar situation. A nightmare?

"You got it last time. This time it *must* be dead—and I gets my share."

Alathea didn't want to open her eyes, because she knew it would do no good. She pushed herself up, scraped and sore from scalp to toes. She squeezed salt water from her shoulder-length hair and croaked, "I'm alive, Hetch. Got a blanket I can use?"

This time Hetch gave her food—raw fish. Ravenous as she was, she could hardly choke it down. He left her to sleep for a long time before he took her out to Find with him. He tied her foot to the boat so she wouldn't jump out again, but she knew now there wasn't much chance of getting out the way she'd come in.

Alathea had been there eleven Tide Turns when Hetch took her to meet more of his people—families who lived nearby in the maze of tunnels and caves. They were odd little folk. Though they talked fish all day, just like Alathea's brothers, there the similarity to anyone she knew ended. They could all see in the dark, and they hated fire, so they ate the fish they caught raw. They had no pottery or metal they hadn't scavenged, and no way to warm the damp caves they lived in except with steam that escaped from cracks in the stone.

Hetch dumped her with Yora, the shy daughter of Munt, his arguing partner. "Papa told me Hetch had a new Finder," said the girl. She sounded sullen, maybe jealous. "Do you got a name besides 'Sea Find'?"

"My name's Alathea, Molly's Tenthchild."

"That name be bigger than you. Do you care if I calls you Thea?"

"Um, no. That would be fine." *Mother would be mortified,* thought Alathea. She'd never had a short name. Her mother insisted that the future owner of Molly's fishing boat have a dignified name. Thea—she liked it. Much less pretentious than Alathea. And losing 'Tenthchild' made her feel more her own woman, less her mother's property.

"I'm s'prised you do so well at Finding, since you're a Blind," lisped the girl.

There it was again. Not just 'you *are* blind,' but 'you're *a* Blind.' And what were Blinds, then—others like herself, washed in from outside? Or were there Under Sea folk who could not see in the dark?

"Who—or what—are Blinds?" Thea asked.

"Sometimes one of us Under Sea folk is born not seeing the light people's bodies make. When we's sure they're really Blind we send them to grow things in the Sinkhole, in the sunlight where we can't go. That much heat is worse than fire—*we* can't see out there."

Sunlight. What she wouldn't give to see sunlight again. Just to *see* again.

"But that's days away, even by boat, and upstream all the way on the Great River," said Yora. "Hetch wouldn't want you that far away—how could he profit? No, he's happy you're so good with the boat." She leaned in close and whispered fishily in Thea's ear, "You should see Hetch's cave full of Finds."

As Thea pulled her blanket closer under her chin, she wondered if there was warm clothing in Hetch's cave. She was *always* cold down here. Aah, to feel the sun on her shoulders. Would Hetch send her to the Sinkhole, where the Blinds lived?

"Don't get no ideas, now," said Hetch. "I'm bringing in twice as many Finds now. Blind or no, you stay here. I get enough Finds, I can afford me a wife, like Munt's."

Yora said, "Hetch, you got more than enough Finds to get you a wife. Any woman in the Under Sea would have you, right now."

Thea shuddered, thinking, *Not* this *woman! You're welcome to him.* She hunkered in her blanket, listening as Hetch and his friends chattered. Fishing and fish spears, merfolk stealing Finds and breaking bridges. "God-cursed merfolk so cold you can't hardly see 'em 'til they're right on you," said Hetch.

It sounded like they really believed in merfolk. Thea wished they'd talk less about merfolk, and more about the Sinkhole, where they sent the Blinds. Upstream, they said, along the Great River. It sounded like another way out of this underground prison. Unless it was just a story, like the merfolk.

A few Tide Turns later, as Hetch led Thea back to the little side cavern she slept in, he pressed several lumpy things into her hands. "So ye don't fall over things so much." He cleared his throat and spat. "But douse it when you hears me coming."

"Th-thank you." Thea's heart started pounding. She waited until she couldn't hear Hetch's slapping footfalls over the drip of water, then lay her gifts on her blanket and felt them, one by one—a crude clay lamp, a tinder box, and a bladder of oil.

The sparks that flew out as she rasped steel over flint were the most welcome sight of her life. But the cave was so damp that the tinder wouldn't light. Cursing in frustration, she tipped a few drops of the rancid oil out, and finally a tiny yellow flame sprang up.

She cupped her hands around it for a moment, imagining it warmed her chapped fingers, then held the lamp up to look at her cave. Black stone, reflecting the light back in places, undulated overhead, down the walls, and underfoot. Her blanket was gray, except where salt stained it white, and her crude wooden mug looked moldy. So she had light, but not much to see. Still, the thought that she *had* light cheered her, so when she slept there were no nightmares of things crawling out of the unseen depths.

After that, she made herself so helpful to Hetch that he started letting her do more and more. Sometimes, she was sure, he forgot she was a Blind—except the day he came up on her unexpectedly, before she'd pinched out her lamp's flame.

"Agh!" he cried, and flung his hands before his eyes. In the instant before she snuffed the light, she saw him—a fish-pale, shabby little man with huge eyes in a pinched face. A few wisps of colorless hair were plastered to his wrinkled skull, and Thea wondered what Yora saw in him.

Thea hoped he found her dark hair and brown skin as repulsive as she found his fishy paleness, so he wouldn't consider *her* as his bride. But even so, she knew she'd better take steps to find the almost-mythical Sinkhole, and escape this damp, dark prison.

So it was that, one day many Tide Turns later, she found herself alone with Hetch's round leather boat. She had counted the number of steps to get from her little cave to the cavern where the tide rose and fell through the Pipes. Hetch had told her that the Great River emptied into the cavern of the Pipes—indeed, she had felt its current—but could she find it, alone in the dark?

She tied saved food and her lamp up in her blanket and carried the boat and paddle out to the big cavern. She lit the lamp, glad of its broad base, and set it in the bottom of the boat. Its tiny light wasn't much help in the immensity of the cavern, but comforted her.

The roar of rushing water echoed through the cavern. Since the only time Hetch, Munt and the other Finders weren't out in the cavern was ebbtide, once she set the boat in the water she had to paddle with all her might against the tide's pull down the Pipes. Thank the gods that the past how-many days of paddling for Hetch had strengthened her arms and shoulders.

The noise of the water changed as she got closer to the other side of the cavern. It echoed and splashed, the rushing roar changing with every swish of her paddle into the water. The boat bumped against the wall, then spun, and she almost lost her paddle. It wasn't working.

But no, the current that spun the boat was water coming into the cavern, not just the tide rushing out the Pipes. She had found it, the outlet of the Great River.

It wasn't easy to paddle against the river's force. Her shoulders burned and her hands were getting sore. There must be side tunnels, somewhere she could stop and rest. But her lamp, in the bottom of the boat, was too small to light the river's edges.

She tried to paddle one-handed so she could hold up the lamp. The feeble light danced off ridged and folded cavern walls, shadows showing cave mouths where none existed when she paddled closer. She was losing headway, the boat slowly turning in the water, when she saw a ledge.

With the lamp back in the bottom of the boat, she focused her attention on paddling. She bumped into the damp stone, scraped along it, feeling with one hand for the ledge she had seen. There. The stone was slippery and cold, but she jammed the paddle against the stone, stopped the boat, and clambered out. She vowed that once she got out of here she'd never go near water—or caves—again.

It felt wonderful to rest her arms and shoulders. She huddled on the ledge, clutching her blanket around her and chewing on the tough semi-dry fish she had brought as provisions.

Behind her, someone said, "Are you a Blind?" She almost slid off the ledge in her startlement. She turned to see two small, pale people shading their huge eyes from the light of her lamp. "Are you going to the Sinkhole?"

"I am." She took a deep breath, happy to hear these folk farther up the river speak of the Sinkhole as a reality. And they didn't seem hostile; maybe they could tell her more. "Why?"

"Can you take another Blind with you? We'll provide well for you both."

"Can he paddle?" She could see the cave mouth they'd come from, further up the ledge.

"Of course he can."

"Then I suppose he can come with me."

The little man pulled Thea's boat from the water. "We'll hang it on the peg here," he said.

The woman took her arm. "Come with me and I'll get Koob and his things."

Thea followed her into the cave and along a tunnel, rubbing her shoulders and massaging her sore palms, keeping her hand cupped around her lamp so it wouldn't blind her guides. Would that Koob needed a full day to gather his things.

The woman stopped. "We've found a boat, Mother. I'll bring Koob in to say goodbye." She patted Thea's arm. "You can rest here; Mother's about gone, and won't mind sharing the room."

Thea sank to the cold stone, exhausted. "Here, take my blanket," mumbled a voice—some old toothless granny, it sounded. "You'll have to come get it though; illness has taken my sight."

Here was one of the Under Sea folk her light wouldn't blind. Thea lifted her lamp and saw a woman—toothless, her eyes sunken—huddled against one wall. The woman turned her head, stared straight at Thea.

"How can you bring me light, boatsman?" asked the woman. "I've been blind these hundred Tide Turns."

"I'm a Blind," said Thea. "I suppose you can see the hotter light of my lamp." She thought she knew what was wrong with this woman. "About your illness—did it start with your mouth hurting, and your muscles sore? And then your teeth fell out, and you lost your sight?"

"You know it did—many of us ail so. Are you a healer? Can you cure me?" The woman's mumbled words became louder, and she clutched at Thea, staring into her face.

"I'm not much of a healer, but I know a cure for your disease—I've seen it in sailors. Can you get fruit or vegetables from the Sinkhole? Even seaweed would help. If you eat those you'll get better, though you'll never get your teeth back."

Someone came in behind Thea—the woman who had led her in. "Nay, 'tis too late for Mother. We have need of her skin to fix the boat, so we won't have to ask others to help us all the time."

"Really, it's not too late," insisted Thea. "She's got scurvy, and fresh fruit cures it, even in a person near death."

"Leave her alone, false healer," said the woman. "She's too far gone. We need her skin and bones."

Thea was confused. They didn't *want* to cure this woman? They wanted to . . . use her skin and bones? She remembered Hetch, the first time she'd ever heard him. He, too, had talked of patching his boat, when he thought she was dead.

She shuddered with more than cold. The ghouls!

Shouting erupted in the tunnel, echoed through the little cavern. "I tell you, that boat's mine! I've come to fetch back that accursed Sea Find of mine."

Hetch had found her.

He burst into the niche where Thea stood, and the woman snarled, "You can have the creature. She's stirring up trouble, telling Mother she'll live when she's dying of the wasting disease."

"Fishguts," Thea cursed. All that hard work for naught, and these people didn't even appreciate her trying to help their mother.

Hetch grabbed her arm. "Come along, Sea Find. And since 'tis your fault, *you* paddles us home."

Of course. Good thing it was all downstream. As Thea climbed into the boat, she could hardly stand to touch it, and wondered of whose skin it was made.

Misery became the one constant in Thea's life. Hetch took her lamp away and she paddled in constant darkness. Then back to the cold damp cave, with one thin blanket to stop her shivering, and raw fish for breakfast, lunch and dinner. *I'll likely get scurvy too, with this diet*, she thought.

Finally she screwed up her courage to confront Hetch. The next day, as they paddled into the big cavern, she asked, "You're doing well enough, with my help. Are you still mad at me for stealing your boat and trying to get away?"

"Mad?" asked Hetch. He didn't sound like he was paying much attention.

"The rags of my clothes are rotting off my body, and I'm going to puke if I have to eat another raw fish. I haven't been warm for as long as I can remember. When will you treat me better?"

Hetch was quiet for a long time. He found something in the dark and fetched it, dripping wet, into the boat.

"That's how Under Sea folk live. Clothes I can get. But nothin's wrong with fish."

"Don't you have fruit or vegetables? Yora says they grow them in the Sinkhole. You'd all do better to eat more than just fish. Yora's sick, isn't she—losing her teeth? Do you care for her at all? Does Munt want her to live, or does he just want her to die so he can use her skin to patch his boat?"

"Talk t'me after we get back," came Hetch's gruff voice, and Thea decided silence best for her cause right now.

Later, Thea huddled in her blanket, tired and cold. Hetch's well-known footsteps echoed up the tunnel, and he entered the cave and dropped to the floor with a grunt.

"I thought 'bout what you said, Sea Find," he said. "For a Blind you done damn good. But you *know* things, know lots o' things. You knowed about Yora. You get around even though you can't see. And I thought, what else do my Sea Find know?"

"I *do* know a lot," Thea answered. "Where I come from, I'm a fisherman. You spear fish, don't you? We catch them, hundreds at a time, in nets. Why, even your Finding would go better with a few nets!" Thea leaned forward, stared at where she thought Hetch sat.

"So, what be a net?" asked Hetch.

Thea knew entirely too much about nets. She had mended them before she was old enough to go out on the boats. She had started netting when she was eight. She had helped throw them out and pull them in ever since. Her mother had seen to that.

"Can you find me a bunch of twine? I'll make a net."

Hetch was quiet for a long time. Thea listened to water drip from the ceiling and sat silently, waiting. Finally he said, "There may be summat in my Find room for you." He took her hand, led her up one of the tunnels in the maze, to a drier, warmer cave than the one she lived in. It smelled of seawater, mold, and spices.

Thea said, "I've got to have my lamp back. I can't find what I need if I can't see."

Hetch grumbled, but he handed her the little oil lamp. "I'll wait for you out here. The heat hurts my eyes," he said. His scuffling footsteps as he paced in the corridor outside counterpointed the drip of water somewhere down the tunnel.

Thea squatted in the smelly cave, lighting the lamp by feel. Then she stood, holding it up to light her way through Hetch's Find room.

What a collection of junk! Most of it was driftwood, such as they collected every Tide Turn—but the piles also contained such treasures as sea chests, tangles of salt-stained fabric, and carved hardwood finials. First Thea found and pulled on a warm knitted sweater—too big but she didn't care—then she picked through ropes and lines, most of them too thick to net with. Finally she found exactly what she needed—a wooden reel of twine, big enough to use for a stool. She wondered how Hetch had ever fit something that bulky into his boat.

She settled in a nest of fabric and started her net. Without a netting spindle, the rough twine tore at her fingers, but Thea worked as fast as she could. When she had knotted a net long enough to hold between her two outstretched arms and drop to her feet she blew out the lamp, stashed it in a fold of her sweater, and called Hetch in.

If only she could see Hetch's face as she showed him how it could scoop up fish, or how it could be anchored somehow near the Pipes to collect Finds even when Hetch couldn't be out in his boat. Was he impressed? Bored?

Hetch grabbed her arm and dragged her down tunnel after tunnel, into a big cavern with water splashing down the center. "There be fish here; show me."

"If you help." She was growing bolder. "You can see where to place it." This was crazy, throwing the net in blind, pulling it out without knowing what—if anything—it had caught.

"Three fish!" Thea thought it a pathetic catch, but for a man who stood in cold water to spear his lunch one fish at a time, it must seem impressive. "Ha! I will be the best Finder in the Under Sea!"

He dragged her back to his caves, the fish dripping against her side all the way. "What needs you—for a big net—for catching Finds at the Pipes?" His peculiar accent, always a little hard to understand, got worse when he was excited. Thea hoped this would impress him enough that he'd start treating her like something besides a slave. As long as it *wasn't* a wife.

"A big net will take a long time. I'll need lots of twine, more lamp oil, and something to make a shuttle out of. And can I work in the warmer cave?"

"Anything! Work fast, and," his voice dropped to a hoarse whisper, "don't tell *nobody*—'specially Munt—what you does."

The hard part of rigging a net near the Pipes was finding a place to anchor it. The Tides were very strong and—as Thea well knew—would tear her big net free if it was not firmly anchored. But Hetch's native cleverness came into play here. He and his people had been working with water and stone for generations. He clambered over the slimy wall at the low tide like some cave spider, pounding in Found spikes with a big rock.

"Ha! Even if Munt sees it, no way he'd be making his own," said Hetch. He held his hands over his eyes and let Thea uncover her lamp and check the net. "Is it good? Is it good?" He sounded like one of the boys that hung around the docks to help unload cargo, back home.

"Looks good, Hetch. Now let's see if it works." The water started rushing back into the cavern, and Thea watched it swirl by for a moment, fascinated, before she covered her lamp again. Then she went back to her normal job, paddling the skin boat while Hetch pulled in Finds from the rushing tide.

She was almost as excited as Hetch, next Tide Turn, to see if there were any good Finds in her net. As the water calmed before the next inrush, they paddled out to the far Pipe, where they'd anchored the net against a wall. "It's still there; most of the spikes held," said Hetch. "And yes, so much here! Heavy Finds, and fish, and—" his voice broke off and she heard splashes and cursing. "Paddle hard, get us away!"

"What's the matter?" Thea asked, already paddling.

"We've netted one of the merfolk. Nemarun, God of Fish, help us."

Thea put all the now-considerable power of her shoulders and arms into paddling the boat. Until now she'd thought the Under Sea folks' stories about the merfolk, how they were fearsome warriors and held grudges, were myths. "Hetch, shouldn't we go back and set it free?" she panted. "If it's grateful to us—"

"Too late! We ain't their friends to start with, and now they be *really* mad."

"But if we—"

"Save yer breath, Sea Find," Hetch growled. "I knows merfolk."

An eerie hoot wailed over the water, then at the far end of the cavern pale blue light blossomed. Thea turned to see three scaled, half-human heads pop out of the water. Each merman held a wicked barbed spear and a pale blue globe. "Now we'll die," moaned Hetch.

"Oh hush," said Thea. "Help me paddle." Somehow the fact that she could *see* made it easier to face the idea of a battle with the merfolk.

"They have us. Nemarun, be good to me." Hetch curled himself into a ball in the bottom of the boat.

"Fishguts," swore Thea. "You coward." A spear struck the boat, cracking one of its bone ribs. Thea grabbed a heavy branch from the bottom of the boat and threw it at the closest merman, who let out an unearthly wail. She paddled away toward the cavern's wall.

A spear ripped through the boat's side, and Hetch screamed, "I been hit!" Thea kept paddling, though the boat was filling with water. Soon she'd have to abandon it. Was Hetch really hurt? Could he swim?

She poked the little man with her elbow. "Hey, are you all right?" He just moaned. She grabbed his thinning hair, pulled his head out of the water. "Listen, Hetch, the boat is sinking. Snap out of it or you're going to drown!"

"Don't lose my boat!" Now he was paying attention.

"They holed it; it's sinking," said Thea.

"I'll bail while you paddle." He started scooping water with his hands, then yelped. "My arm!"

"What?" Thea paddled as hard as she could, but the boat moved sluggishly.

Pain sliced across her left shoulder. She gasped, but kept the boat moving. Hetch screamed. "They're all around! They're everywhere!"

In the blue glow from the globes floating on the water's surface, Thea saw four, maybe five scaled bodies coming at them through the water. She swung her paddle, hit another merman, then headed for an opening in the wall directly in front of her. If she could only reach it before the merfolk overwhelmed her.

Her paddle and the merfolks' tails and spears splashed and churned the water. She didn't seem to be making much headway, but they hadn't got her yet, and the boat hadn't sunk. Then a rock thunked into the side of the boat. The merfolk hooted again, to be answered by raucous shouts, and rocks that splashed into the water all around her. Hetch's people were throwing rocks at the merfolk.

She paddled until the boat hit the cavern wall. Arms seized her, grabbed Hetch, pulled the boat from the water. She was dragged back from the opening, and wrapped in a scratchy tangle of blankets.

"Lie still now, and I'll tend that cut," came a soft voice. It was Yora. Thea lay back, content to let someone take care of her for a change. Her back and arms ached, and a sudden sting in her shoulder made her draw in her breath with a hiss.

"Hetch is hurt bad," said Yora, as she bandaged Thea's wound. "Stabbed in the gut, he was, and right through the arm. Mam's tending him. Likely he won't make it—and now where will I find a husband?"

People marched in, laughing and chattering. "Ha! Routed them!" "We'll teach merfolk to mess with us Under Sea folk."

"Ho, Sea Find!" Munt squatted beside Thea. She turned her head away from his fishy breath. "You've proved a hardy Underseaman. What'll you do with all Hetch's Finds?"

"Wha-what do you mean?" asked Thea.

"He's dying, Sea Find. He's got no kin but you. After the Tribute, his Finds is all yours. You're a cursed good Finder; you can be rich!"

Not likely I'll stay here! Thea's head swirled—with confusion, fatigue, or the pain of her wound, she wasn't sure which. *I can go home. I can leave, get warm, go back to the sunlight.* Not back to fishing, though, no matter what her mother said. She'd had enough of cold and damp, and never wanted to eat another fish in her life.

But Munt was still talking. "And when Hetch dies, his skin and bones is yours," he said. "Them merfolk beat your boat all up. You'll need a good hide for patching it."

Gathering Shards

Lasai leaned against the trunk of a tipil tree, his legs folded beneath him, his hands loose on his thighs. A breeze fluttered the leaves, and the tiny brass cymbals Lasai had hung in branches throughout the grove rang in a constant ting-a-ting-ting. These movements, varied but constant, trembled at the edges of his vision.

The barest translucent flicker of white, different from the silvery shiver of the leaves, brought Lasai back to himself. He shook the red silk cord tied to the tree branch above him, and the cymbals ting-tinged in rhythm. The white grew, solidified, became a young female Ebchian clutching a tiny one to her bony breast. Her lips drew back from her fangs in agony, and she limped badly as she followed the cymbals' seductive music—food and ease for her soul—into the grove. By the time she reached the tree next to Lasai's, the translucent white had given way to golden tan, and he could hear the chuff, chuff of her labored breath. So she'd died quickly, and didn't know she was dead.

"Come, come, come," chanted Lasai, shaking the cymbals in the tree again. "Hear what I have for you. Ease for pain, ease for sorrow. Ease for anger, ease for fear. Come, come, come."

The Ebchian stopped and raised empty eyes, eyes that slowly gained color and vitality and sentience. "Fire from the sky," her voice came, nearly unintelligible. "Running, terror, pain. Must protect my hatchling."

The tiny Ebchian, a mere wisp of white until then, stirred as a golden blush swept over its insubstantial body. "Papa," it called, even less aware of its death than the mother. "Where is Papa?"

A Seeker, thought Lasai. *No doubt running through ruins, looking for her mate as the fire came down.* Seekers were hard, as reunion was required before they let go. But this one was strong, and should draw the beloved as the cymbals' blessed music had drawn her.

Lasai spoke again, in her language, a language dead before his race found this planet, but familiar now from all the sad and anguished tales he had heard. "Come, rest, ease your hurts while I seek your mate."

The Ebchian sank to the grass beneath the tipil trees, revealing the ugly burn across the muscle of one thigh. Lasai rang the cymbals again, and the Ebchian closed her eyes briefly. When she opened them, the wound had disappeared. Lasai nodded his approval.

"We were so hungry. Kelchet crept out after dark to sniff for something to eat. He never came back that night, he never came back that day, so I went to find him. I had to bring Talknor along—he's barely hatched, too small to care for himself."

Lasai tugged the red silk cord, the cymbals chimed, and he nodded and nodded. "Yes, yes," he murmured.

"What horror we found! The Assembly gone—naught but rubble and a crater. The houses all broken, the people. . . ." her voice faded.

"Yes, yes." The tipil leaves flickered like blinking eyes.

"The only people I saw were dead. Bodies, all bloody and torn, right there on the street. Nothing alive—not even scavenger neki. I hid. I gave Talknor water from rain puddles so he wouldn't squeak. I heard nothing, but I *felt* . . . I felt the Enemy watching." Huge golden eyes stared into Lasai's.

"I followed Kelchet's odor as well as I could, in the dark and the rubble. He'd gone to the Market, but it was destroyed. Blasted so thoroughly I couldn't smell anything edible left."

Ting-ting-a-ting.

"He'd gone to the Residence after that. It was not crushed like the other places, but was empty, cold, odorless. The Crystals were gone from their sockets. Kelchet hadn't lingered; nor did I."

Lasai asked, "You followed Kelchet. Did you find him?"

She keened, a high-pitched sound that overlaid the cymbals' easing ting-ting with pain and terror. "The Enemy came in their spaceships, their odor like fire. Their machines ate houses and people alike, and spat flame. I ran, with Talknor, though their weapons burnt my leg. And then it was fiery, so hot. . . ." She waved her muzzle from side to side in distress.

Lasai pulled the cord and the cymbals chimed. "So, so. But it's over now," he soothed. "Continue your search. Find Kelchet."

The Ebchian turned, sniffing eagerly. "Yes! I smell him. He is near."

An opalescent glimmer at the grove's edge coalesced into a tall golden-brown Ebchian who grew more substantial as he ran toward the female. Lasai relaxed against the trunk of the tipil tree, pulling the red cord and watching the tender reunion of alien ghosts dead for a thousand years. Aah, much joy here to leaven this planet's burden of pain and terror. A Seeker satisfied was a strong positive force. "Come, come, come," Lasai chanted. "Join forever. Rest in peace and joy."

Intent one with the other, the golden hue of the ghosts' skin faded, the definition of muscle and bone blurred, and translucent wisps drifted toward Lasai and the chime of cymbals. They touched him, one, then the other, then the tiny awareness of the child. Warm and cold at once, a chaos of alien hopes and pain and being. Lasai took chaos into himself, held it, cherished it. He closed his eyes and felt the otherness tingle through him. Then the souls were gone to promised peace, and the small residue of their lives added to the essence of thousands of their brothers and sisters integrated into his body and mind.

Much later he opened his eyes. He leaned, as always, against the tipil tree with legs folded beneath him and hands loose on his thighs. Exhausted. Leaves fluttered, cymbals chimed—and something else moved, at the edge of the grove.

A being, its skin ghostly white, eyes too small, body too tall and too thick. No. Lasai shook his head. A human, one of his own kind. A living woman, not a ghost, staring at him pale of face, with eyes shock widened.

"Wha-what *were* those things?"

He did not comprehend for a moment, had to taste and smell the words, turn them over and examine them. He had not talked to a human in seasons, and human words were buried deep in his memories.

She spoke again. "Were those . . . Ebchians?"

His hands twitched and he took a deep breath. He pushed himself unsteadily to his feet, clutching the tipil's trunk to keep from falling. Remembering human manners, he offered the woman a hand. "I am Lasai. How do you do?"

"I'm Melny van Dam. I'm an archaeologist in the city northeast of here." She took a deep breath and asked again, "*Were* those Ebchians?"

"They were."

She waited, probably expecting more. A tall woman, and slender. Her dark hair was tied back with a piece of string, and she was clad in a rumpled coverall and shouldered a bulging daypack. Now that her color had returned, her skin was sun browned almost to the amber shade of the Ebchians.

"They tell me in the city that you know the language of the Ebchians, know the names and locations of their cities. Is this how you learned. . . ?" Her voice trailed off. Then she squared her chin. "Were they *ghosts*?"

"Yes," said Lasai calmly. "I offer them ease. The people of this world died in pain and fear, and until they have peace this world will suffer."

"So . . . do you know *how* these people died?"

"They had an Enemy, which came from space with fire and death."

"What was the enemy?" she asked eagerly, leaning toward him. She was taller than he. Though it had eased many souls, his body was small, and had drawn in upon itself over the years until it was compact and wiry.

"They did not know, so I do not know." He felt for the emotion behind the woman's words. Curiosity and eagerness, but strongest, though buried, deeply and unacknowledged, was fear. "What do you fear?"

"You see it!" Her breath quickened, and she grasped his hand
between hers. "No one else believes. 'It happened a thousand years ago.
These races are extinct.' Yes, the Ebchians are extinct. But what of their
destroyers? They were not of this world, of that I am convinced. What
do I fear? The Enemy of the Ebchians."

"I do not know the Enemy," said Lasai. "I know people and places,
cities and lives. The Orb King ruled in his Residence in shining Ashlent
an hour's walk from here. Mothers sang lullabies; youngsters sang
hunting songs. But they are all of this world. Nothing else has come to
me. Perhaps no Enemy died here. Perhaps their souls do not yearn for
peace. I do not know the Enemy."

"*How* do you know all this? From ghosts? Most people . . . usually
I would say. . . there *are* no ghosts!"

Lasai shrugged. "You have seen. I have felt. I draw them with my
cymbals and they come to me, hungry for peace. I feed that hunger. They
give up anguish and fear—and they are a talkative people. They tell me
things. Thus I learned their language."

Melny crouched a little, face to face with Lasai. "How can *I* learn
this?" she whispered.

"You have seen. Most people—even you archaeologists—cannot see
the Ebchians. Since you see, perhaps you can feel their sorrow and their
joy, partake of their lives. For it will take this for you to learn of them."

Her mouth opened, but no sound came out. She stood, face drawn,
gaze elsewhere. "I don't know if I can," she told him, and strode quickly
from the grove.

Lasai leaned against the tree, gazing at the spot where Melny van
Dam had disappeared. She would return. There was much curiosity in
her.

He left the tipil tree to prepare a simple meal in the hut he had
rebuilt from a ruin.

Though archaeological methods change over the years, one thing
always remains—the need for the trowel, the fine brush, the human touch
for the fine details. Melny van Dam crouched within a sturdy plastic hut,
erected to ward off the chill of winter and protect the artifacts she was
uncovering. She brushed away shards of plaster, dust and soot and
stared at what she had found. A skeleton. Around hugely elongated
bones, a plethora of tiny, fragile ones, like chicken bones, all lying within
what could be sections of black armor. Not an Ebchian. A riding beast?
A draft animal?

Fear prickled down her back. This thing was so strange, like
nothing else they'd found on Ebchi. The placement of bones, the

symmetry, all were different from any other creature on the planet. Could it be the Enemy?

She licked dry lips as she stood to set up the holographic imager. The fear that had ridden in the back of her mind for so long was in the forefront now, and could no longer be pushed aside. *I have found the Enemy, and it is a strange and alien thing.*

Fewer ghosts came in the short cold days of winter. The beauty of winter was different from that of the warmer months, and attracted ghosts with different needs. Lasai felt something stirring in the blasted cities, and waited patiently in the grove.

Days had passed when no ghosts answered the call of the cymbals. Snow had fallen, blown about, then melted. Today a warmer wind melted the cymbals from their icy prisons. Unease built around Lasai. He waited. When a blue gleam began to coalesce at the edge of the grove, he knew his waiting was over.

Then came the slap of wet leaves against boots. Melny van Dam. Lasai raised a hand to warn her off, then forgot her, watching the form building before him.

It was very tall, attenuated arms and legs jointed at odd angles. A head that seemed much too large for a slender neck. Shiny black armor—or was it an exoskeleton? A row of eyes gleamed around its forehead.

The more solid the creature's form became, the stronger the despair that lapped from it to fill the grove. Despair muffled the cymbals, choking Lasai and bringing tears to his eyes.

The creature cried out three harsh syllables, in no language Lasai had ever heard. It staggered toward him, catching its limbs in the tipil branches, pulling free, crying its desolation.

In the way Lasai had learned the Ebchian language, he began to know the meaning of this creature's words. 'Kekzh hch i[click].' *They are dead.* But this was no Seeker. The very depth of this despair told Lasai that no beloved family would appear to ease this being.

Lasai pulled the red cord and chanted, "Come, come, come."

The creature stopped, clenching and unclenching pincer-like fingers. "Khaaa," it grated out.

Melny van Dam, crouched in the soggy leaves beside Lasai, gasped. "Is that it? Is that what I found?" she whispered.

The oval head tilted, the row of shiny eyes looked at her.

Lasai blinked. Just as with the Ebchians, Melny van Dam saw the being—and it saw her.

The creature lifted its arms to the sky and cried, "Kekzh hch i[click]!" The strength of its emotion battered at Lasai, tore at his mind.

He rang the cymbals, but their little music was no balm for the desolation that flowed from the being's soul.

Lasai pushed himself to his feet and dropped the blanket.   He spread his arms wide, made his body a focus for the flood of despair. The world of Ebchi would never have peace until this being knew ease.

Fingers touched his. Melny van Dam had risen with him. Now she grasped his hand and added the strength of her young body and mind to his.

Abruptly the creature collapsed, its sticklike limbs folding compactly as it crouched. It turned the smooth oval of its head to Lasai and spoke, as the ghosts always did, their fear and pain tumbling out in words. If on one level they were only gratings and scrapings, on another he knew their gist, if not an exact translation.

"They are dead, they are gone, and all the warriors of Chchkek are undone. They are gone, our Mothers, to the littlebeings, the unknowing, the singulars. We are dead, though we breathe. We are dead, though we fight. If the Chchkek are to die, so will the littlebeings, all the singulars." Its pincer fingers clawed the wet leaves, dug grooves in the earth beneath the tipil trees. "They are dead!"

"Hs, hs, find ease," soothed Lasai. "That was long and long ago, a thousand cycles of the sun."

"We are of the Void—we die beneath the sun. We die of the heaviness. Oh, we die."

Melny van Dam's hand trembled in Lasai's grip, and he risked a glance at her. Her face was white and taut with strain. When he loosened his grip on her fingers, though, she shook her head.

"Before the Chchkek die, the littlebeings die. The killers of the Mothers." The creature rose to its spectacular height once more. "The Mothers are dead!" it keened.

So. The Enemy—the Chchkek—destroyed the Ebchians because they had killed some of the Chchkek. And by so doing, the Ebchians had doomed the entire race of Chchkek? He puzzled at that a moment, then put it aside. What was important now was that he had met the Enemy, face to face. As he had told Melny van Dam, to face fear is to conquer it. This was no longer a faceless Enemy, but a being who sorrowed as the Ebchians had.

Lasai raised his arms again, one hand still linked to Melny van Dam's, and took a half step toward the Chchkek. "Find ease," he chanted. "Find unity. Lose the weight of the world and join your soul with others."

The Chchkek's long, clumsy limbs, no doubt graceful in the void between worlds, came together in a clash of shiny black. "No weight?" For the first time since its appearance, the constant flow of despair faltered. "Join?" It bent, its pincer hands very close to Lasai and Melny's faces. But the shiny hardness dimmed as the creature contemplated Lasai's words.

"Come, join, become one." Lasai groped with his free hand for the red cord, and the ting-ting of cymbals resumed.

"The Mothers. . . ?"

"Are in everything." Now Lasai trod an unknown path. Whoever this creature's Mothers were—queens, matriarchs, or goddesses—Lasai could not know if the Chchkek reverence for them was religious, actual, or a combination of the two. But the answer seemed to please the creature. Its lonely desolation slipped away, smoothed to a wave of longing that no longer choked.

"Come, come, join," urged Lasai.

The creature placed its ungainly limbs carefully about Lasai and the hardness lost definition. The black outline faded to a glimmer of blue that drifted toward Lasai, touched him with a chill worse than the coldest winter day.

Then that chill deepened to the cold between the planets. The Chchkek awareness, so long separate, sought others of its kind but did not find them. The remnants of the beings Lasai had eased made a unity of aliens, littlebeings, creatures with no facility for sharing thoughts and purpose. And yet . . . and yet. . . .

An image of a Mother built itself in Lasai. A being whose deep caring came from the residue of a thousand lives. This *one* doesn't matter. This single body is part of the totality of Chchkek . . . the totality of Ebchian . . . the totality of humanity, of sentience.

Lasai had eased the souls of the Ebchians, given them peace, but traces of love and caring—and grief and sin and guilt and fear—remained with him. Now the Chchkek awareness sought to find in all that vast storage space of Lasai's body an echo of a Mother of the Chchkek.

And found that echo—once, again, a thousand times.

The young Seeker with her mate and hatchling sharing love. An old Ebchian's pride in her hundreds of descendants. A youngster looking back at his parents as he left to fight the Enemy. Shared love—with each other, and with—

No! The part of Lasai that had become Ebchian cried out in horror. This was not one with them, soft and golden, small and bright of eye. This tall shiny black intruder: reject it!

Pain washed from Lasai's head down his spine, along his bones and nerves to the tips of his fingers and toes. Lasai the human had accepted the Chchkek, but the part of him that was now Ebchian had not. A babble of memories—all the hidden hurt and rage that Lasai had taken in with the good—rose to choke him. The Chchkek ghost, bewildered to find a semblance of a Mother and then lose it, swelled in Lasai's mind.

He was not strong enough! The Chchkek sought to crush him, to make him pay for the loss of the Mothers. Feeling, sound, sight ebbed as Chchkek anger waxed within him.

Melny shivered, the strangeness of what she was witnessing—what she was *living*—almost overwhelming.

How could she have known, when she took the old man's hand, that he would draw her into this wash of emotion and memory? It was heady, this knowledge of a long-dead race. But the Enemy, the Chchkek, might destroy all! What could she do? How could she help?

She was too aware of her surroundings, the cold-shriveled trees, the trampled mud and leaves, the old man's hand shaking in hers. She closed her eyes to shut out external stimuli. She must find it, must *fight* it.

The strength of the Chchkek's grief and anger washed over and through her. She took it into herself, cherished it as she tried to understand. What did Lasai do to ease his ghosts? *He* did not fight.

As the Chchkek had opened to her, now Lasai's mind and heart joined with hers. She found in him the needful things, the ways to soothe, the ways to take in the myriad uneased hurts of the dead.

So, so. The soothing calm Lasai usually spoke ran now unvoiced along Melny's nerves. *Everyone has had pain, but now all hurt is gone. Let it go, as it should have gone before.* The pain of a master's beating, the agony of the Enemy's fire. This time, with Melny an integral part of the easing, Lasai did not need to cover over the hurt. Melny knew it would do no good to merely soothe it with balm and leave the hurt there, buried. She gathered the pain, cherished it even as it seared her nerves and muscles. She accepted a mother Ebchian's grief as her hatchling died under falling rubble. The crushing agony of a great machine tearing out life ran through her own bones. The hurts, large and small, washed through and out of her body. And she knew Lasai did the same, for she was one with his mind and soul, and the anguish drained through both of them.

Last to go was the great despair of the Chchkek. As the ghost faded to peace, a whisper in the grating Chchkek language said, *Even singulars are joined, united. We did not know. We did not know.*

A red eye of sun burned through the clouds at the horizon. Rising wind clanged the cymbals. A gentle hand wiped suddenly freezing sweat from Lasai's forehead with a blue bandana. Melny van Dam.

"Did . . . you feel? Did you know?" Lasai's voice was barely more than a croak.

Wonder transfigured Melny's face. "How could anyone know? All that's there in other beings, all the joy and pain and love and hate, and so much more. It hurts, oh, it hurts, but to *know*. . . ." Her voice trailed off. She blinked down at him. "Are you all right? Should I call the doctor?"

"I've always survived this before." He shook his head a little, though it hurt to do it. Her eyes were too large but too few. Her head the wrong shape, rising at an awkward angle from that thick neck. Flat face, tiny teeth, what is this creature?

"This has happened to you before? You *are* a crazy old man."

"Well, never quite like this." He closed his eyes to still the double vision. He must hold on to his humanity, not become just another spark of consciousness among the memories.

Melny held a cup to his lips. "Here, drink this. You must have sweated off liters. When it's gone, I suppose I can melt snow, if there's some still around. Yes, there at the edge of the grove. . . ."

He opened his eyes when she gasped. On the edge of the grove a wisp of white writhed, gathering substance to form the translucent shape of an Ebchian.

"Another ghost?" asked Melny.

"Yes, an Ebchian. But—" this was no sorrowing civilian killed all unaware by the Chchkek war machines. The hate and fear and terrible, terrible guilt flowing from this ghost was stronger even than the desolation the Chchkek had emanated.

The Ebchian drifted into the grove, never solidifying, passing through the branches and seeming unaware of the ting-ting of the cymbals. His death had not come quickly; the ghost's face was horribly disfigured, his body burned and twisted.

"Come, come," rasped Lasai. How could he ease this tortured soul, weak as he was from accepting the Chchkek? And yet, what better time, now that he had cleansed himself of the hate and pain he had held onto from those thousands of hurting others?

Lasai groped for the red cord; Melny found it and placed it in his hand. Her face was drawn and pale, but the look in her eyes was transcendence, not fear. She took his other hand and held it tight.

The wind died as full dark descended on the grove; now the cymbals in Lasai's tipil tree were the only ones sounding to attract and feed the ghost. Ting, ting-a-ting. How tiny and pitiful the sound was against the horror of this ghost's past.

It stopped partway into the grove, the ruin of its face rippling; sometimes translucent, sometimes blackened and twisted— and a few, just a few, glimpses of the golden skin this ghost had worn in life.

"Find peace, find ease," chanted Lasai. The ghost's blind head turned, back and forth, as if seeking. But he was no Seeker. No, he was something very different. "Come, come, lose pain and fear and guilt."

Guilt. Lasai had not known the word in Ebchian until it came from the left-behind memory of one of the many he had eased. But this ghost knew it. Suddenly color rushed into its form, and it sank to the frozen ground in a crouch, no longer a twisted ruin but a strong young Ebchian. A soldier.

Ting-ting-a-ting.

The ghost spoke, as the cymbals—or Lasai's presence—seemed to compel him. "We did not know."

Lasai drew in a sudden breath, echoed by Melny van Dam. This young Ebchian warrior had echoed the Chchkek's last words.

"We don't like fighting. But as we traveled between worlds they, the Enemy, found our ships and destroyed them. So a horde of us—hundreds!—took our little ships and went to find the Enemy. They were many, a huge sphere of strong warrior ships. We were desperate, and fired and fired on a few of their ships even as they destroyed us. We broke the sphere, and rushed within. They were so big, and we so small and fast, that it was hard for them to hit us.

"Within the sphere another ship—big, different, heavily armored. We thought that here their warleaders must be, so all of us that were left fired on it, rammed it with our own ships until it was nothing but shards floating in the Void.

"The few of us left thought the Enemy would destroy us for that. But they did not." The Ebchian stopped. He was fully substantial now, a tall young male whose amber eyes glowed with purpose.

The echo of the Chchkek's keening grated in Lasai's mind. 'They are dead.' The left-behind memories told him there was no warleader in that protected center ship, but the Chchkek Mothers and their children.

"All firing stopped. We cheered, thinking the Enemy confused by their leaders' death, and sped home in our tiny ships. Our mistake. Their confusion didn't last long, and they followed us, followed us here to our bright and beautiful world." The guilt almost overpowered Lasai, and Melny, beside him, gasped a sob.

Then the flood of emotion changed. The ravages of flame appeared again on the ghost's visage. "We destroyed one ship. They killed us all." Rage overlay the guilt, suffocating in its intensity.

The things Lasai had learned from the Chchkek responded to the Ebchian with their own emotion—a shadow of the despair that had nearly overwhelmed Lasai before. Words flowed from him before he could stop them—the language Ebchian, the thought Chchkek. "By killing the Mothers you destroyed the Chchkek as surely as if you had vaporized every ship of the Community."

The Ebchian's head came up, his eyes glowing in the ravaged face. Lasai had never feared a ghost before, but the rage that emanated from this one chilled his soul. Melny's hand in his trembled; then her body, as she moved closer to him, warmed the unearthly cold.

Not much of a being remained with an unquiet ghost—usually little more than emotion, the unfinished business that kept it from peace. Could Lasai reason with this warrior? Would *explanation* give him ease?

In his calmest, most soothing tone Lasai said, "The Chchkek protected the center ship because it contained the Mothers and all their undifferentiated young. When they died there was no way for the Chchkek to reproduce. Their warriors could have no children. They had no planet base."

But Lasai's words did not soothe. The semblance of scorched flesh left the young warrior's visage and he stood whole and vibrant in his rage. "We sought but to protect our own. The Enemy followed us and killed us. What happened to my people? As I escorted refugee ships away from Ebchi, the Enemy came. My last memory is of falling to earth in my burning ship."

Melny's hand gripped Lasai's tighter. Lasai could not tell the young warrior that his people had all died a thousand years ago. The ghost's rage and guilt were almost more than he could bear; emotion blinded his eyes, stole the breath from his throat, and crushed his body back against the rough tipil trunk.

"Where are they? I searched and could not find them!" A branch tore from a nearby tree, the cymbals tied to its twigs clanging a death knell as it fell to the frozen ground. An unnatural wind whipped through the grove and tore up huge chunks of earth and winter-killed grass, then mixed them with soggy leaves, twigs, and branches. "Where? Where?"

Lasai's soothing voice was lost in the wind's howl, and the cymbals offered no ease. A branch tore a gash in his cheek and the earth beneath his feet trembled.

Melny rose to her full height, clutching Lasai's hand in a painful grip. "So you're going to kill *us* now?" she screamed over the wind. "Hasn't a millennium of restless anger on a wrecked planet taught you anything? Neither you nor the Chchkek were right, and millions of innocents suffered for it. But it's over. It's done. Let it go. Take Lasai's ease and go to the peace you deserve."

The Ebchian may not have understood her words, but he felt the impact of her emotion. He turned toward her, his ghostly form swelling to far more than the meter-and-a-half he had owned in life.

Lasai struggled to loose his hand from Melny's grip. The ghost shouldn't be aware of her, should only know him. But it was too late, and the Ebchian was upon them.

The cold between the stars had chilled Lasai when he took the Chchkek's consciousness into his mind. But the Ebchian was all rage and fire, heat that seared skin, muscles and bones. *Is this how it feels to die by fire?* Worse than the physical pain was the agony of this being's mind. The Ebchian cried out for those who had died in his sight—too many, too many—and for those others who had died alone. All because of him. Because he had led the Enemy to his world.

We celebrated, cried his pain. *Then the fire came, and we died.*

Then a calm voice, soothing. Melny van Dam. *Yes, you died, and so did the Enemy. All are gone now—but there is still life on your bright and beautiful world. Look around and see!*

The ghost, within Lasai, within Melny, used their two minds to look at the grove: wind-torn trees and soggy earth in the cold dark of a late winter night. But the Melny-part noted flickers of moonlight shining on the icy branches. The Lasai-part heard the sleepy ting-a-ting of cymbals in the dawn breeze. Memories of the grove in summer, cool and green, sweet-smelling and filled with music.

The Ebchian's rage tried to drag old hurts to cover the beauty. There were none. Lasai had purged them. In the same way pain and terror and guilt flowed away from the Ebchian through the seared channels of an old man's mind, through the fresh young body of the woman.

Last came the Ebchian's regret: that he had died so young, that he had never had a chance to love his children, to dance again in the rain, to smell the great living wonder of the world.

The ghost faded.

Bright sunlight and the tinkle of the cymbals, ting, ting-a-ting. Lasai eased Melny's head from his shoulder and climbed to his feet unsteadily. The grove smelled of melting snow and thawing earth, and there were fewer branches torn from the trees than he'd thought.

"Did he find peace? Or did he just go away?" Melny sat up, raking damp leaves from her hair with dirty fingertips.

Lasai felt within himself, and realized even he was unsure. "I don't know. He—he was strong, and the pain—"

"Should we stop digging? Is that what's waking these things?"

"No. These souls need their peace. But the strong ones—I don't choose when they come. Can I withstand them?"

"I will help."

Help. Lasai had never shared his self-imposed task. He had come from far to complete this task, merely because he knew he must. But he was losing his strength, getting old. *Could* Melny help?

"I felt it, I understood what they were saying." The note in her voice was exultant. "This is like nothing I ever imagined. *Sharing* lives of folk dead a thousand years, knowing their feelings. We took their pain and grief, and we purged it. We did it together—didn't you see how we helped one another?" She looked around the grove with wondering eyes, seeing, he thought, more than the winter-killed leaves, the soggy ground. "My fear is gone with all the rest. The Enemy is gone—and I sorrow for them too."

She had seen and heard and felt. She spoke truth.

Melny van Dam sat in the grass of the tipil grove, her legs folded beneath her. Beside her, so close that his knee brushed hers, the old man, Lasai, sat with hands loose on his thighs.

This sharing, this knowledge—this was what had driven her to study anthropology, to take up archaeology. This urge to know of others and how they lived and thought and *were*. She had found it in such a way!

She and Lasai sat, outwardly still, inwardly sharing—no longer singular. Cymbals chimed in a breeze that swept the scent of spring to beings almost as appreciative as the Ebchians had once been. A wisp of white coalesced on the edge of the grove, and the two-voiced chant began. "Come, come, find ease, find peace."

Power Sources

Dry grass rustled against Hallelujah Tuckett's legs as she squatted in the shade of a cotton tree. She wriggled her shoulders, wishing she could scratch where the sweat was trickling down. But she had better things to do with her hands. She wouldn't let a little itch stop her from learning the magic.

Tlakh, the Boon witch doctor, would dump her quick if she didn't pay attention. Tlakh made it clear he didn't care if she was an offworlder—she was just another apprentice to him. Halley was determined to be a good apprentice. She knew Tlakh's tales were magic—hadn't he cured her flu in about five minutes?

With the other apprentices—rusty-furred Pellag, Jhiweel of the golden eyes, and tiny Suftek—Halley watched taleweaver Tlakh's movements. The long gray fingers of his left hand swooped toward his right, caught a loop of string, and pulled back. He tipped his hands so the apprentices could see. "Tchon."

"Tchon," Halley echoed with the apprentices, copying the movement with the red yarn looping her own hands. *A hammock*, she translated to herself. She followed as he bent his index fingers over a set of loops and twisted his hands. "Ekha troon, the rising sun."

Halley copied his every move, grunting with satisfaction when her completed string figure looked like Tlakh's. "Kazha mokee," said the taleweaver, and Halley thought *a water hole*. The figure looked like a round, deep pool—and she could change its depth by moving her index fingers.

While Tlakh helped Jhiweel, who kept twisting the string the wrong way around his hands, Halley, Pellag and Suftek practiced the figure. When Tlakh was satisfied, he said, "Now my story." As his long fingers manipulated the string, with movements graceful as dancing, his story unfolded. "The hunter wakes in the dark, stretches and climbs out of his hammock. He is thirsty, so he goes out to fill the water basket. The sun rises as he walks toward the mountains. And there, in the plain, is the water hole, deep, full of cool water." Halley was glad his words were simple ones. She actually understood him.

At the story's end the apprentices sighed their appreciation. Halley never understood the point of Tlakh's stories, but she knew there was more to taleweaving than just stories.

The taleweaver dropped the loops from his fingers and returned the string to its place around his neck. "Now, Khallee," he told her in heavily accented English. "Look at our braids."

Pellag sidled up, her long nose twitching in nervousness, and gave Halley three braids, each carefully tied at the end and decorated with a bead, as Halley had shown them. As Halley turned them, checking for how tightly and evenly the braids were made, the apprentices crowded close, breath whistling between their teeth in excitement. "This one's too loose—see how the strands separate? The other two look fine."

"Do you think you could braid skekki fur?" asked Tlakh. "To show us how you get braids all over?"

"I'll try." Halley didn't like teaching, but it was worth it for the magic. Shy Suftek ran out into the compound, caught one of the long-haired beasts, and brought it to Halley. The skekki settled into her lap, making comfortable heh-heh noises, and she began combing the tangles from its fur.

"Do you tell a tale as you braid?" asked Tlakh, watching intently as she separated out strands.

"Uh, yeah, sure." Since he expected it, Halley began one of the stories her mama used to tell her, changing it a little for the Boons. "My mama, Glory, used to tell this tale. Ol' man, uh, wererabbit wanted a wife. So he went to a hunter's camp while the hunter was away and asked his wife to come live with him. 'I've got a great pot, full of khip roots and meat every day.' The wife was hungry, so she went away with ol' man wererabbit." As Halley talked her fingers flew, making a braid in the animal's long fur, tying off the braid with colored string and a bead, and starting another.

"But after a day in ol' man wererabbit's den, she saw no great pot, and got only grass to eat. She knew she'd made a bad mistake. But she was far from her band's territory, and didn't know how to get back to the camp. So she said to ol' man wererabbit, 'You've shared your den and your food. Come to my camp, and I'll make dinner.' Ol' man wererabbit eagerly ran back to the camp, and the woman followed. 'Gather wood while I dig khip,' she said, and ol' man wererabbit did. She filled her pot with water, and when ol' man wererabbit came back she popped him in the pot, sealed it with ghatt sap and leaves, and built a fire under it. When her man came back from hunting she told him she'd caught wererabbit for dinner, and he never knew what happened."

Half the skekki's fur was braided now, and she stopped and looked up at Tlakh. He stared at the braids, his long nose twitching. "You do this with all the hair on a khuman's head?" he asked.

Halley nodded, forgetting that didn't mean 'yes' for the Boons, and the bells and beads in her braided hair clicked and jingled together. "Yes."

This seemed to puzzle Tlakh. "Your strings are different and your tales are different. I do not yet understand khuman taleweavers."

Tlakh lifted his hands, signaling an end to the lesson. "We will finish the braids, and when you come back you can tell us if we did well." The apprentices covered their faces with their hands and backed off.

Tlakh put one of his long-fingered gray hands on her shoulder and drew her away from the knot of apprentices. She followed the taleweaver through the dusty courtyard, dodging skekki, into a hut half hidden in the cotton tree grove. The air was cooler there, but it was dark and a little stuffy, and smelled of spices and dung.

"Khallee, some of the Eblekh Zai—not of Ghuxi band—are unhappy that we learn from each other." Tlakh rubbed his hands together, back and forth. "You must stay away for a time."

"But I want to learn the tales!" Halley protested. *And the magic*, she thought but didn't say. "You said you'd show me how to make a proper string."

Tlakh sat carefully on the pounded-earth floor and fumbled in a pouch that hung from his belt. "I have not taught you enough yet. But you can practice. Collect dead fibers like these." He brought out a handful of what looked like fur.

"Okay," she said, "I'll collect dead fibers." She squatted in front of him, watching his fingers.

"Roll them against your hip, and keep adding more fibers." As she watched, squinting in the dim light, a long piece of twine grew under his fingers against the smooth leather of his shorts. His fingers moved almost too quickly, feeding in the bits of fur.

"Can I try with some of yours?" she asked, not sure she could make string like that.

The twine dropped to the floor when he hesitated. Quickly, Halley bent and picked it up. She rolled it on her hip; the tiny hairs prickled against her palm.

Tlakh's nose quivered, and his hand moved forward, as if to snatch the string back from her.

"I add more fiber to the end?" she asked, and held her hand out to the taleweaver.

He stared at her for a moment, then pressed a wad of fur into her hand. "Add it a little at a time; it must twist in with the rest of the string."

Halley's end of the twine was lumpy, but held when she pulled on it. "I will practice."

Tlakh smoothed his heavy mane and turned away. "Be careful. I have not taught you enough."

Halley paused where the dirt track met the paved starport road to pat dust from her legs and give the small of her back a good scratch. Behind her, heat shimmered from the plains and the gray-green bushes.

Ahead, sun glinted off the polarized windows of the Grayplain Port Tower and the shiny plastic sides of businesses and homes.

Clean, bright-colored shops lined the starport's broad avenues. The contrast with the filthy, crowded streets of Asher city, back on Tufar where Halley grew up, had enchanted her the first day. But that was before she realized that *nothing* ever happened in Midway's Grayplain starport.

Halley wrinkled her nose at the ozone and chemical smells wafting out the door of Trisha's Hair Care as she entered, but welcomed the air conditioning.

Round, comfortable Trisha looked frazzled today. She was busy rolling a perm and called, "Good timin', Halley. 'Most everybody called in sick and that guy wants cornrows." She pointed at a man lounging in one of the waiting chairs, poking idly at the newsscreen.

"Late in the day for that," said Halley. "Does he know how long it takes? Might not be time."

"So ask him. Looks like he's got heavy pockets; prob'ly tip good. And you're fast."

Worth a try. The quicker she earned money, the sooner she was off this planet. Halley strode over. "You the guy who wants cornrows?" She looked at his shoulder-length hair. "It takes a long time."

"I've got time," the man said. "I owe myself something nice. I've been going crazy. You wouldn't believe how busy Starport Authority offices have been, with half the personnel out sick. Give me the works. I like beads; got glass ones?"

Halley washed the man's hair, thinking, *You got it good in the 'Thority offices, brother, even if you are busy now. Bet you make ten times what I do.* She parted out three strands and began to braid. "Lotta sickness there, huh? Must be the season. We were down to skeleton crews at my other job this morning."

"Yeah, and my boss is an ogre. Sheela DeGraff may look and talk good on the newsfeeds, but in real life . . . whew! When she wants something *now*, it doesn't matter *who's* out sick."

Several hours later Trisha walked by and tapped her arm. "Like we don't got enough trouble already, Halley, there's one of your Boon friends hanging around outside."

Halley began another braid, her fingers never pausing as she craned her neck to see out the door. Humans in the starport called the natives 'Boons' because they looked a bit like Earth baboons. The one squatting just outside the door was skinny, his iron-gray mane unkempt. Halley didn't know him; his cheek tattoo was three green triangles, tip to tip. Tlakh's band all had two red circles, like teardrops, tattooed beneath their eyes.

Boons didn't often come into the human starport. Some of the bands wanted the offworld imports, others barely accepted the humans' presence, and a few bands plain hated offworlders. But none of the Boons seemed comfortable in the plastic-and-steel environs of the starport.

"I've been out with Ms. DeGraff to see some Boons in their compounds," the man said. "It's incredible that they choose to live in such primitive conditions."

Halley grunted. She'd found that no one on Midway but her anthropologist friend shared her fascination with the Boons.

When Halley finished the man's braids, it was closing time. She stepped back to admire her handiwork. "Take a look," she told the Authority employee, handing him a mirror.

He inspected his hair, turning this way and that so light flashed off the glass beads on the braid ends. "Looks great!" He pressed a five-mark into her hand, flipped his card into and out of the payment slot in the front counter, and left.

One five-mark more toward leaving this place, she thought.

Trisha followed him to the door and locked it behind him, then turned to face the shop, empty but for staff. "Listen, folks," she said to the beauticians, who were sweeping up cut hair and putting away bottles of shampoo. "This is bad. Starport Authority is shutting the shop down to check us out. Too many of the clients are getting sick—stomach aches, headaches, stuff like that—and 'Thority wants to know why."

"What'll we do?"

"We run a clean shop!" the staff protested. Halley wondered if the guy whose hair she'd braided had been here to check out the shop. She almost wished she'd tossed his five-mark back at him, but that would be stupid. She needed every mark—especially if Trisha's place closed down. Without the extra money she earned here, she'd be stuck on Midway forever. She didn't make enough as a forklift driver to pay for a ticket offworld.

"I'll call you when I find out more. I'll prob'ly be here all day tomorrow, showin' guys around while they take samples for their tests."

Halley stood outside the door for a long time, staring at magenta and blue, pink and turquoise shops without seeing them. People getting sick after coming to Trisha's? Why would such a thing happen?

She shook her head, heard the click-click of the beads in her hair. Tlakh would know what to do. No matter what Sarah, her anthropologist friend, thought, he wasn't just a storyteller, and his stories and string figures were more than entertainment. He'd cured her flu, just three sendays ago.

The Meng Brothers Storage and Transfer warehouse echoed with early morning footsteps. Halley yawned and looked at the schedule posted on the break room's wall. A big cargo ship hung in orbit over Midway, and the first shuttle load of goods should already have arrived. Halley dropped her lunch sack into her locker and opened the door into the main warehouse.

A babble of uneasy conversation washed through the door, echoing from the warehouse's high ceiling. Halley's fellow workers milled around, gesturing at empty docks and sealed bay doors. Halley elbowed her way through the crowd to join a knot of workers clustered near the bay door. A notice taped to the door read, 'As of 0600 all space traffic will cease due to planetwide quarantine. Orders of Grayplain Starport Authority.'

"What the. . . ?" She turned to her nearest neighbor, skinny Floyd Ross. "What's the story on this?"

"Plague's what I heard."

"Plague!" Halley repeated. "I don't believe it." But the authorities had closed down Trisha's Hair Care.

"Twenty people called in sick yesterday, thirty-three today," said Floyd. "Same thing happening all over town. My wife stayed home from work with a headache and a fever, and both my kids were throwing up this morning." Worry creased his forehead, and he licked his lips again and again. "Couldn't get a doctor appointment, and no one can get in the clinic door, it's so crowded. Don't that make you believe?"

"So there's flu going around. That's not a plague. I was sick a few weeks ago, but I'm fine now. . . ." She remembered how Tlakh had chosen carefully from among the strings around his neck, how he had recited one of his pointless stories and formed a string figure. Instantly her nose had stopped running, her sinuses had cleared, and before she left the taleweaver's compound all symptoms were gone. That was when she started believing that Tlakh actually worked magic.

She asked Floyd, "Anybody die?"

"Two or three," he said. "And some people have been sick for a week or so now, delirious or in a coma."

The babble of conversation hushed, and Halley turned to see the hardwood door at the back of the warehouse, the one that led into the office complex, open. A man in a crisply-starched tunic, one of the Management bozos, stood with his hand on the lockplate as if to assure himself he could leave quickly. He cleared his throat and said, "I, uh, see you've found the notice."

A growl of comment filled the warehouse. "Damn right!"

"What's goin' on?"

"*Is* it plague?"

The guy waited, pulling nervously at his lower lip, until the noise calmed down. "Due to the inordinately high number of cases of serious illness, Starport Authority has closed the port and an investigation is underway. There must be no possibility of an infectious agent being transmitted off the planet by spacers contracting the illness. All ships that have left the planet within the last two weeks have been contacted by overspace comm and will be placed in quarantine upon arrival at their destinations." The Management guy pulled at his collar as if it were too tight, his eyes darting from face to face.

Halley's fellow workers shuffled their feet and muttered to themselves. Finally one spoke up. "So what we gonna do? You gonna lay us all off? We gotta eat."

"Yeah."

"You said it, man."

The Management guy cleared his throat. "Meng Brothers Storage and Transfer will see to it that you and your families are cared for. Company doctors will open a clinic in the break room and you will be allowed to draw against future earnings if you need cash before the quarantine is lifted."

"All right!"

"Not too bad."

"Maybe old man Meng got a heart after all." That might make the other workers happy, but Halley knew what it meant. No pay until another ship came in, and any money they drew from Meng Brothers would put them that much further in debt. She'd indentured with Meng Brothers for three years to get off that scum-hole she used to live on—but she didn't want to stay here a day longer than those three years.

"Go home now," said the Management guy. "The clinic will open at about fifteen this afternoon."

A hullabaloo of questions met this statement, but the Management bozo had already slipped back through the heavy door to the safety of the Meng Brothers offices.

"I'm not goin' home," said Floyd, still standing beside Halley. "I'm gonna call Mina and have her bring the kids, and be here when that clinic opens." He pulled his mem from his pocket. Others must have had the same idea; mems were coming out all over the room.

"You do that," said Halley. "I'm leavin'." No job, no work at Trisha's. Maybe she could find spacers, trapped on this dustball by the quarantine, who wanted their hair done. Or maybe Tlakh would talk to her, even though his people didn't like her taking magic lessons from him. He'd be mighty interested in a plague that had half the humans in the starport down sick.

The street outside the warehouse was nearly empty. Heat shimmers danced over the pavement, and the spacers arguing on the corner wore nothing but shorts. Halley started down the alley between Meng Brothers' warehouse and Nguyen Manufacturing's offices, and nearly tripped over the Boon crouching in the shadows. "Hey!" she said, rummaging through her mind for something to say in his language.

The Boon started to run, in that odd hunched-over way they had. The three-triangle cheek tattoo, and the broad scar on his shoulder, made him pretty recognizable. He was the Boon who'd been outside at Trisha's.

He got something to hide? Halley thought. This would be a good excuse to go see Tlakh—maybe. He'd have an idea why this guy was following her, or watching her, or whatever he was doing.

Two apprentices stared at Halley from the intertwined branches of the ghatt tree walls of Tlakh's compound. The spicy smell from leaves they crushed wafted down to her as she stood impatiently waiting for the gate to open. She listened to the muted chatter of voices and 'heh-heh-heh' of the skekki, wondering if Tlakh would ignore her, leave her standing out here. *He knows I wouldn't come here except for a good reason.*

Finally, she heard thongs unwind, and the gate swung toward her. Tlakh himself stood framed in the entranceway, his long nose quivering.

"Uh, Tlakh—hey, I know you don't want me back so soon, but I've gotta ask you something." Halley didn't want to spend a lot of time on welcomes.

"Khallee, what is it you wish to know?" Tlakh could be equally blunt. He fingered the grubby strings around his neck.

"Two things, actually. First, have you heard about the sickness in the starport? Nobody can come or go in the skyships."

Tlakh's fingers stilled, twined in the strings. He drew air through his teeth in a prolonged hiss, then let it out explosively. "Khallee, this could be a trouble between your people and my people."

"You think, even though all the docs say we can't pass germs back and forth, that we might? I mean, could we have caught this from you—or could we pass it to you?"

"It is not that, Khallee." He paused, sorted through his strings, then pulled one over his head and threaded it between his fingers.

"You know what this is then?" As usual when she came out into the plains to see Tlakh, she was sweating in the heat. A droplet tickled down her forehead, but she ignored it, intent on Tlakh's answer.

"You have not *caught* it from us," he answered, his eyes intent on the figure he formed. His fingers flashed through the moves so quickly Halley could hardly follow them, much less recognize and name them.

He pulled his hands apart, displayed between them a completed figure she had never seen before—a network of diamonds. After gazing at it for a few seconds, he dropped the strings from his outside thumbs and pulled gently. The figure disintegrated into a single loop around his hands.

He placed the string around his neck and looked at Halley. "You had a second question?"

"Uh, yeah." She squatted in the dirt, found a twig, and drew the triangle pattern she had seen on the scruffy Boon's face. "One of your people—from another band—has been watching me in the starport. He had this cheekmark."

"Green triangles?" asked Tlakh, squatting and pushing his head forward at an angle a human neck could never duplicate.

"Yes. He had a wide scar on one shoulder, like something had burned all the hair off."

Tlakh tipped one hand from side to side, the Boon equivalent of nodding. He stood abruptly and grasped Halley's hand. "Come, I will teach you."

Halley followed Tlakh quietly, confused. She scuffed through the dust into the cotton tree grove in the center of the compound, trying not to trip on the long-haired skekki scampering underfoot, and very aware of Boons, young and old, staring at her from their huts and hammocks. The taleweaver took her to his hut and motioned for her to sit on a low leather stool.

"Have you practiced making strings with dead fibers?" Tlakh asked, squatting before her on the hard-packed dirt.

She had used cuttings swept from the floor at Trisha's. Making string must be trickier than it looked. "I practiced, but my strings turned out full of thick and thin spots, and pulled apart when I tried to make figures."

"Always practice with dead fiber. Use living fiber only for the tales you wish to make real."

The intensity of his words, spoken carefully in English, told Halley that this was *important*. But so far she couldn't figure out what the importance was. She went over his words in her mind, setting them and their tone so she could ponder them later. Now if only she knew what dead and living fibers were!

"I have taught you easy tales, ones an apprentice can do no harm with. I cannot give you stories of great power, but as you are a khuman taleweaver, and you have shared your weavings with me, I will give you weavings that could help you."

He's trying to tell me something without coming right out and saying it, thought Halley. *Or else he just can't figure out how to say it in*

English. She wished she could understand him better, and read his body language.

Tlakh sorted through the strings around his neck, pulled one grubbier than the rest over his head. He quickly arranged it in the most common opening, tchon or 'the hammock', and looked at her expectantly. She felt through her jumpsuit pockets until she found the old piece of red yarn she used to practice string figures, and followed his lead.

"This is a hunting tale," he began. "The hunter leaves her hammock and wanders through the plains." He dropped the string from one hand, took it up again in a different pattern. "She looks into wererabbit dens, climbs ghatt trees, and goes up and down hills." She copied his complicated actions, hampered by the fact that her pinky fingers were less flexible than his far thumbs. "Finally she gets to the mountains, and there she finds her prey." Halley had to take loops of string off her fingers with her teeth to 'get to the mountains.'

Tlakh extended his hands for her to view his final product—three diamonds linked at the points, framed by more string. He smiled. "Now catch your prey."

Halley stared at the figure, her brow furrowed. Her figure wasn't nearly as even as his. Catch her prey?

"Put your string down and I will show you."

She slipped the string off her fingers, carefully straightening it.

"Put your hand through the middle mountain."

She did, and he dropped the strings from one hand and pulled them tight around her wrist. "Caught!"

Halley laughed. It was a child's trick, his hunting tale. She freed her hand from his string, took hers up again. Slowly, they went through the motions, the tale. "Now you catch me!" said Tlakh.

Halley was right-handed; she dropped the strings from her right hand. They slithered across Tlakh's wrist, and he stood free, smiling at her. "What's the trick?" she said, even more mystified.

"Watch closely, Khallee." He whipped through the figure again, and she placed her wrist in the central diamond. He loosed the strings from his *left* hand, and trapped her again. "Do you see?"

"I do." She slowly went through the figure, came up with diamonds. Tlakh put his hand within her loop, she released, and her string closed around his wrist.

"The power of a living string will help you catch your prey. See, I hunt lizard." He took a dried lizard claw from the little pouch at his waist, handed it to her, and formed the figure. She pushed the claw through the center diamond, and he caught it with the string. "To hunt wererabbits, I use their fur or bones. It is stronger if the string is animal, not plant. Do you see?"

She stared at the taleweaver, breathing in little gasps. "Yes, I see. I see!" The truth of it was blinding. What did Sarah, the old anthropologist, call this? Never mind its name, but to catch a rat, use something from the rat. Living string—could that be a string made from the fur or hair of a living creature? Her yarn was polyester—never living, and therefore safe for practice. But what would have happened had she used those strings she tried to make out of hair swept off Trisha's floor? That was 'living' hair.

No wonder her cornrows fascinated the Boons. Wouldn't hair still attached to a person be even more alive than cut hair?

Tlakh took her hands between his. "What do you use for power, khuman taleweaver?"

She didn't know where to get power—she still didn't have it all figured out. She gaped at him, her mind racing.

"You have few power sources in your skyship compound," he continued when she could not answer. "Do not use up your own energy."

My own energy. Make a string from my own hair? Maybe I could braid something, make it long but thin enough.

Tlakh loosed her hands, sat back on his haunches, and formed the hammock. "How many tales can you learn today?" His fingers flashed through a figure, his lips moving as he watched the string. "I can show you well-being, healing of stomach ills, the healing I did when you came to me sick that time."

"Yes, the healing. That would be good." She picked her string out of the dirt, formed the hammock. And something came together in her head from the ideas and knowledge swirling there. "You only heal, right? You never do this to, like, *give* people stomach aches or stuffy noses. *You* would never do that."

Tlakh caught her gaze with his. His eyes, luminous like an alley cat's, bored into hers. "No, *I* would never do such a thing. We proper taleweavers would not do such a thing."

"Show me healing, then."

The phone light blinked in Halley's dark apartment when she got home. The message, from Trisha, said, "Hey, Halley, the powers-that-be decided the shop was okay, since the whole starport's down sick. We'll be open tomorrow, if you want work."

Hmmm. Halley wanted the money to add to her off-this-boring-rock fund, but she was more interested in the puzzle of Tlakh's magic. The *stories* aren't important, like Sarah the anthropologist thinks, it's the string figures. And just as important is what the string is made of. Maybe, Trisha, it *is* your shop causing the sickness. No *proper* taleweaver would make people sick—but what about an improper one? A scruffy one, with triangle cheekmark and a big scar on his shoulder?

Halley dug through her junk drawer and found a cord to replace her filthy, unraveling piece of yarn. While the cooker heated her dinner she ran through the healing figures until her fingers moved almost as smoothly as Tlakh's. She practiced the hunting figure, taking a spoon in her mouth and pushing it through the center diamond. She didn't want to forget the figures while she decided how to use her knowledge.

Few customers showed up at Trisha's the next day. They were subdued, and all talk was of the starport closing and the quarantine. But there weren't many beauticians, either, so Halley was busy.

After her stomach had cursed her out for hours, she finally went to the back room to heat her lunch. She sat at the little table, eating rubbery reheated wererabbit, and stared out the window. She could see the corner of 5th and Plainview Ave., but there wasn't much scooter traffic. The back door of Poczwardowski's Bagels opened, and a boy carried a sack of garbage out to the public waste slot at the end of the alley.

The boy went back into the bagel shop, and a gray figure rose out of the shadows in the back of the alley to poke a long hairy arm into the waste slot. It was Halley's old 'friend', the Boon with the triangle cheekmark.

Halley eased out of her chair and touched the door's lockplate. The door opened silently, and she stepped into the street, between the Boon and the alley's opening. "What do you think you're doing?" she asked.

The Boon whipped around, darting toward her faster than she had expected. "Hey!" She snatched at his arm as he passed. "I need to talk to you!"

He pulled away violently, knocking her off balance, and ran. She landed hard on her butt, her breath whooshing out. When she scrambled to her feet and ran out of the alley, he was gone.

"Damn." Halley opened her clenched fist, looked at the few long hairs clutched there. Hairs. She reentered the alley and inspected the waste slot. More gray hairs clung to the lip of the slot, where he had pulled his arm out quickly. She gathered them with a grim smile. She had become a hunter, and now she knew her prey.

As she walked home that evening, her smile was gone. She needed a string of living fiber to tap this planet's power. She didn't want to cut her own hair; besides, Tlakh had warned her against that. He had said plant fiber was usable, though not as strong—but what would living plant fiber be?

Surely the taleweavers had a source of plant fiber. What? She stared unseeing at the bright pastels of the shops around her as she strode home.

In the residential areas, the colorful wall panels of houses were interspersed with the gray-green of native foliage. Here were plants, but what could she use to make a string? Not leaves or flowers, and if the Boons had some way to use the bark, she had no idea what it was.

She paused beneath the sketchy shade of a young cotton tree. Cotton trees. The well-protected center of Tlakh's compound was full of them. Of course! Their cottony seedpods were harvested every year. In fact, Halley had a cushion on her bed filled with the fluffy 'cotton'. She'd made it herself, with cotton harvested from the tree behind her apartment building.

She ran the rest of the way home, burst into her apartment, and grabbed the cushion off her bed. After she wrenched the stitches open, she pulled out the soft cotton; it clung together in long strands. She tried rolling it on her thigh and it twined easily into a string. She added more fiber, rolling it in, trying to keep it smooth so it would be strong enough to make figures. No time to get fancy. 'Triangles' might be long gone, scared away when she'd recognized him.

How dare that slime make everybody sick! If Tlakh were not her friend, hadn't been willing to teach her the Boon language and, later, the taleweaving, she'd think the Boons were out to get humans. But Tlakh *had* said some of his people didn't like him teaching her. Was Triangles one of them?

Finally, about two meters of string held when she tugged on it. She bound the ends together and threaded it between her fingers. It was rather too soft, hard to use. But it held.

She pushed the string into her pocket, palmed the door open, and ran out into the quiet evening street. She'd try it at Trisha's, where he'd been at least twice before.

The back door recognized her palm, even though the shop was closed and dark. She pushed it open and left it, then dragged a chair over to where she could see out, but no one entering the alley could see her.

She lay the Boon's hairs, tied with a bit of thread, on the edge of the table. The cotton tree string clung to her fingers but she formed the hammock, then dropped the string from one hand. "It's early morning, and I jump out of my hammock. I'm looking for 'Triangles', but he's not in my compound. I wander through the plains, but can't find him. He's not hiding in wererabbit dens. I find a stand of ghatt trees, but he's not in their twisty branches. Up and down the hills I search, but don't see him." Halley pulled loops over her fingers with her teeth; fibers escaping the string tickled her upper lip and she nearly sneezed. "Long past breakfast, long past lunch, tired and hungry, I get to the mountains. And there he IS." She coaxed the string into the final pattern of three joined diamonds, picked up the little bunch of hair with her teeth, and poked it through the middle diamond. She released the strings from her left hand and coaxed the soft fibers down around the Boon's hair, tight. "CAUGHT."

She wondered how long it took to work. Give him at least a half hour—it took her that long to walk to Tlakh's compound. In the meantime, it wouldn't hurt to try the figure again. Tlakh had said the magic of plant fibers wasn't very strong.

"Caught." Halley completed the figure for at least the millionth time. It was full dark out, and the only things she'd seen for hours were the lights of occasional scooters. Her shoulders ached, her hands were sore. What had ever made her think *she* could work Boon magic? So Tlakh thought her a taleweaver? Maybe, because she braided hair, he'd mistaken her for someone who knew something special.

Her stomach growled, and she dropped the string to the table. "I hope there's something to eat in the fridge," she muttered. She palmed the refrigerator door, peered into the dimly lit confines. Pickles—they wouldn't make much of a dinner. Bread—moldy.

A scuffling noise outside the door brought her upright, her night sight destroyed by the refrigerator light. She closed the fridge and felt her way along the wall. Slowly, her sight returned.

Skills honed by years in the slums of Tufar came in handy now. As the figure stepped hesitantly through the door, she grabbed him, flipped him, and pinned him to the floor.

His wrists and arms were covered with wiry hair. It was a Boon, but was it Triangles? She couldn't tell—he struggled too hard for her to let go his hands and feel for the scar. Halley knelt on his shoulders to hold him down while she reached for the scissors she'd left on the table.

The Boon stopped struggling as soon as she snipped the first handful of hair from the back of his head. He moaned and went limp. *I guessed right*, she thought. *He's like that guy Mama tells about—Samson.* She slid the scissors along his head and sheared more of his scruffy mane. As he whimpered, she touched his shoulder, felt the broad scar there. She had done it: she had drawn Triangles to her with Boon magic.

"Now I have your hair and I know what to do with it," she said in badly-accented Boon. "Will you tell me about the sickness my people suffer?"

He gabbled something, too quickly for her to understand.

"You've been in the starport a lot; I bet you understand English," Halley said. "I'm Hallelujah Tuckett, and I'm a human taleweaver. What's your name?"

"I am Gezzet," said the Boon. He started to struggle again.

"Hold still so I don't hurt you, Gezzet. Now tell me, why are you making my people sick?"

Gezzet was smaller than Halley, but he heaved himself upward, trying to fling her off. She dropped the scissors and clutched what long hair was left in his mane. She tried to grab his wrist, pull his arm behind him to hold him down, but he managed to get to his primary knees with her still astride his back. He lurched forward, and she conked her head on the table.

"Ow!" She scrabbled for a better grip on his arm, but he jerked away, knocked her over and surged to his feet. He was out the door before she could grab the back of his legs. She'd never find him in the dark.

Halley rubbed her sore forehead, then got up and closed the door. She looked at the cotton tree fiber string, then at the pile of Boon hair. Should she try again, or was this enough?

Halley spent the rest of the night trying to roll a string from Gezzet's hair, the way Tlakh had showed her. The cotton tree fiber had been easy, but the Boon's coarse hair did not cling together.

Maybe braiding would work better. Just use the longest stuff, hold it with a hair clip, and add hair in all the time, like french braids. Once it was long enough, she could tie it around a chair leg, and get a really small, tight braid. Would there be enough?

The greasy, rank-smelling hair would not cooperate. This wasn't like doing hair at Trisha's, where she had . . . wait a minute! She could use setting gel to stick the hairs together.

Halley blinked eyes gritty with lack of sleep when a ray of sunlight filtered into her room. Her shoulders burned with tension, but she had finished two meters of braid. She sealed the rest of the hair into a plastic bag labeled 'Triangles', then bound the ends together and formed the hammock between her hands. The hair string was oddly springy, reluctant to form figures. She didn't want to use it wrong; didn't know *what* to do with it, truth to tell.

After a hot, dusty walk to and from Tlakh's compound, where she talked to the taleweaver, Halley stopped at Trisha's. Gezzet crouched in the alley behind the shop.

Halley halted, blocking his way. She was bigger than he, but last night he had shown unexpected strength. What could he want with her now?

"Zhettal talk you," Gezzet said, rising and stepping forward.

"Who's Zhettal?" She raised her hands between them, and he backed into the shadow of the bagel shop.

"Taleweaver Fekho band."

"Does he want me to come with you to his compound? I'm warning you, I've given your hair to a taleweaver who knows what to do with it, so if anything happens to me. . . ."

The Boon's gray skin blanched, and he collapsed at her feet. "I apprentice Zhettal. Hold my power you."

"Oh, get up. I'm not gonna hurt you. Just take me to Zhettal."

Gezzet led Halley out of Grayplain's shopping district, skirting the execs' walled estates on the west edge of town rather than going south through the tenements, as she did to get to Tlakh's. So Gezzet's not the rogue taleweaver, Halley thought. She was a little nervous to go, alone, to Zhettal's compound. A Boon willing to make a whole starport full of humans sick might not care if one forklift driver disappeared into his compound, never to be seen again. Her hold over Gezzet better be enough to keep her safe.

After a ten-minute walk into the plain they came to a compound. The ghatt trees forming its walls were huge, their branches so intertwined that Halley wondered how the guards found a way through them. The smell of their leaves, in Midway's hot sun, was almost overpowering.

Zhettal's family and apprentices stared at Halley as she followed Gezzet into the compound. Zhettal's hut was in the middle of a cotton tree grove. Was that the usual place for a taleweaver? He—no, she—stood in the doorway, a tall Boon, skin wrinkled, hair almost white. She had many more strings around her neck than Tlakh carried.

Halley felt a moment of panic. What could she say to this woman? How could a warehouse worker make an alien magician stop what she was doing? Halley didn't even know if the Boon spoke English, and her own knowledge of Boon was pretty meager.

Be bold, Tuckett, she told herself. *Put her on the defensive.* "Are you Zhettal?" she asked the old Boon.

"I am Zhettal, taleweaver to Fekho Band. Your name, khuman?" Her eyes met Halley's; she was exactly Halley's height. And she spoke English as well as Tlakh did.

"I am Hallelujah Tuckett, a human taleweaver." Halley had only two strings around her neck—her practice cord and the one she'd twisted of cotton tree fiber. But she would not let Zhettal intimidate her. Here she was *the* human taleweaver, not a forklift driver or Glory's youngest kid. "I've come to tell you to stop making the humans sick. I know what you're doing, and I want you to stop *now*."

Zhettal continued to stare into her eyes, but Halley wouldn't let the old woman make her nervous. "Come into my hut, Tuckett," said Zhettal. "I have talked to many khumans, but none of them carried strings. Perhaps *you* will understand my problem."

Her hut was larger and cooler than Tlakh's, but just as bare. Zhettal squatted in the packed dirt, and Halley sat cross-legged, facing her. "My tale is short," began Zhettal. "I do not welcome khumans to our land, but wish them no ill. Some of my people like the things you give us. Some fear your skyships, and say you will drive us to the mountains, away from our fields. At first I told them this could not be, but then khumans came to the elders. They wanted our fallow fields, to make your compound bigger. Our chieftain allowed this. But now khumans want more. They want my compound." The Boon fingered the strings around her neck and her nose twitched.

"My compound has been here four generations," continued Zhettal. "My cotton trees are strong. I can move my animals. My family can build new huts and hang new hammocks. But my cotton trees keep Fekho band's crops healthy. You are a taleweaver, you understand."

A breeze whispered through the leafy canopy outside the hut, and Halley imagined bulldozers pushing the trees over. Of course. Plant strings—living fiber—for plant magic. Somehow it all worked together, and Zhettal's trees were more valuable to her and her band than anything humans could give her.

"I understand."

Zhettal twisted her hands in the strings around her neck. "I have said no and no and no, but still they come, saying they will give us more things. But what good are *things* if the crops fail and my band starves?"

"Did you tell them this?" asked Halley.

The Boon tipped one white-haired hand. "Many times."

"So you sent Gezzet into the starport to find human hair, to use it against us?"

"I did it to make you khumans go away. No one listened, and I feared when I said 'no' too many times they would stop asking and destroy my compound anyway."

"So you don't hate us, you just want to keep your compound safe?" Halley had a glimmering of an idea. "I think I can help you. But you must work with me."

Zhettal's taut back relaxed, and Halley knew the Boon had been as nervous as she. "Can *you* save my compound? They come back in four days for my answer."

"I'll do what I can." Halley took her practice string from around her neck. "But you'll have to teach me some new figures, for this to work."

When Halley got to Trisha's shop late the next morning, it was empty of all but restless beauticians. "Business not too good?" Halley asked.

Trisha flopped into one of the chairs. "This quarantine's gonna ruin my business. Nobody wants to spend money on their hair when people are dyin' like roaches and they got no work."

"Hey, I got an idea. How about we do a 'quarantine special,' and give people a discount? Something's better than nothing, right?" Halley looked around at the other beauticians, who nodded but looked dubious.

"Okay," said Trisha, "but we can't afford to advertise, not now. A sign in the window would be okay, but. . . ."

"If you'll let me use customer records, I'll do it myself. I'll just pick the rich ones—the ones this quarantine's not hurting."

Trisha's round pink face lit in a smile. "That's the spirit. Catch the Management and 'Thority types. They're not paying wages now. They can afford it."

Halley had learned a few things back on Tufar, before she got away from the squalor of Asher City. She could plant a nice little ad, not too flashy, in selected clients' newsfeeds. A little color, to make them notice it, and just the right message. Saving money, yeah, something about boredom? No. The word 'healthy', since everyone is hyped about sickness.

Business picked up the next day. Though she spent most of her time making cornrows, Halley helped the other beauticians, too—mostly by sweeping up hair after the half-price haircuts. None of the long strands made their way into the waste slot out back, though—Halley sorted the hair neatly into plastic bags and hid it in her locker.

Short ends of hair covered the carpet in Halley's room, and more of it poked out of the bags piled on the bed. Halley sat cross-legged on the floor, dabbing setting gel on the long strands of wavy blond hair she was braiding. This was her prize--hair from Starport Authority's second-in-command, Sheela DeGraff. If she could sway DeGraff. . . .

Finally she had a usable string. It was sleek and shiny, easier to work than the string she had made from Gezzet's hair. She threaded it over her hands, formed the hammock, and slowly began a story as she formed a figure.

"Zhettal gets out of her hammock one morning, stretches, and looks toward the sun. She looks past the cotton trees in the middle of her compound, past the ghatt trees surrounding her compound, to the khuman skyship compound." The figure was one of many diamonds—like the one Tlakh had made once. She dropped two strings from her fingers and began a new figure.

"Aah, the khuman compound is growing, getting close, too close. They want to cut down the ghatt trees, cut down the cotton trees, drive Fekho band from their fields. So, I say to DeGraff, go away from my band's fields and my compound. There is free land to the east of your skyship compound. There is free land to the north of your skyship compound. Turn your eyes from my compound." The final figure was a different net of interlaced diamonds, more vertical than the earlier ones. Halley had adapted it, over nights of trial and error, from Zhettal's figure meant to scare wererabbits from her band's fields.

The sun beat down on Halley's head as she stood outside Zhettal's compound, waiting for the gates to open. Around her neck hung seven new strings—just a few, but the hair of Port Authority or Management types had gone into their making.

Zhettal pulled the gate open herself, her long nose quivering. "Tuckett! Your people will be here soon."

Halley looked at the Boons peeking from huts and hammocks, watching her with curiosity. "Let's go to your hut," she suggested.

The Boon raised one hand, tipped it side to side. "I understand." Her luminescent eyes caught the sunlight and shone as she peered at the strings around Halley's neck.

In the dim, still heat of Zhettal's hut Halley squatted and drew the strings from around her neck. "Here is a string from Sheela DeGraff." She held up the sleek blond loop.

The Boon tipped her hand side to side. "She it is who speaks with me most. 'No' I have said to her. 'No and no.' But she does not listen." Her nose twitched and her extended hand trembled.

A child poked its head into the hut and gabbled something in Boon. "The khumans are here, Tuckett," said Zhettal. "What will you do?"

"I have a go-away tale. I'll stay here in the hut and tell it while you talk to DeGraff." Halley arranged herself cross-legged on the packed dirt and looped DeGraff's string over her fingers.

Zhettal met the humans—a woman in a crisply-starched red jumpsuit and two men in executive gray tunics—in her cotton tree grove. A child spread mats for them to sit on, but the humans declined. "Well, Zhettal, have you made a decision yet?" asked Sheela DeGraff.

The men left the talking to DeGraff and stared curiously, pointing at the Boons and their huts and hammocks. Halley recognized one of them by the cornrows in his hair. She had done them herself.

Halley took a deep breath and moved back farther into the shadows of the hut, hoping they couldn't see her sitting there. She started the figure. "Zhettal gets out of her hammock. . . ."

"As always, Zheela DeGraff, I tell you no," said Zhettal, standing straight and looking DeGraff in the eye. "This compound has been here four generations, and Fekho band needs it."

"We'll replace this town with plasti-homes somewhere else on your lands. We can give you anything you want—clothing, food, even running water piped into your homes!"

"We do not need your *things*. There are other places for you to build your new compound. Go ask other bands."

"But the execs want to expand in this direction. Your chief has agreed to trade some of Fekho's land, and your band is moving farther west—you can move with them." DeGraff put her hands on her hips, her gaze wandering from Zhettal to the huts outside the grove. Halley thought she saw the woman's nose wrinkle.

Halley worked the figure again and again. She wasn't really paying attention to it anymore, just murmuring the tale and moving her hands, forming a net of diamonds, changing the net.

"Zheela DeGraff, I say *no*." Zhettal pushed down with both hands, the strong form of 'no'. "My cotton trees, my ghatt trees--these do not grow in a season! How many seasons will you feed us, until the trees are grown again?" Zhettal's nose quivered, and she twined her hands in the strings around her neck.

Please, Halley prayed. *This has got to work*. If Boon magic could make humans sick, Boon magic should change DeGraff's mind. But how long would it take? Zhettal had to see this work so she'd give her strings to Halley.

Sheela DeGraff shook her head slightly, put her fingertips to her temples. "We can give you fertilizer and growth compounds to help your trees grow. If we promise to feed your people, Zhettal, will you give us your land?"

"The foods you khumans like are not healthy for Eblekh Zai."

"So we'll give you the kind you like, for heaven's sake." DeGraff shook her fists to emphasize her frustration.

Zhettal backed off a step and stared into the open doorway of her hut. Halley didn't think the Boon could see her, but she held the figure up as she worked it.

DeGraff turned away from the Boon. "Fekho band isn't interested in plasti-homes, fine food, all the other things we offer." It wasn't a question.

"No." Zhettal pushed down with her palms again, and stayed looking at the ground, her shoulders hunched.

"Your chief will be angry that you will not let us build on your land." DeGraff rubbed her eyes and shook her head again.

"He understands."

"We will offer all these fine things to some other band, and your band will go without."

Zhettal drew air through her teeth in a long hiss, straightened slowly, and looked DeGraff in the eye again. A smile lit her hairy face. "May another band *want* the things you offer."

DeGraff beckoned to the two aides, turned on her heel, and walked out of the compound. Zhettal watched the three humans get into their scooter, a curious expression on her face.

Halley put DeGraff's string around her neck and ran out of the hut. "It worked! Zhettal, it worked! She left, and she doesn't want to destroy your compound!"

"You are a strong taleweaver, khuman Tuckett." Zhettal looked at the braided strings around Halley's neck curiously. "Tuckett, will you teach me how to make these strings?"

"Will you bargain? I want back all the strings you're using to make my people sick. Let me deal with the khumans from now on." Halley looked into Zhettal's eyes. She didn't feel like a mere laborer, but an equal with the old taleweaver.

"I will give you the strings." Zhettal started to sort through the strings around her neck, then stopped and caught Halley's gaze. "You are a taleweaver of power. Fekho band would be happy to have you."

In all the months Halley had worked with Tlakh, he had never offered to admit her to his band. "I'd have to think about it. Your chieftain will accept this?" Halley asked.

"*I* choose new taleweavers. There will be no problem." Zhettal dropped her eyes and twined her fingers in the strings around her neck. "But I must ask something else."

"What's that?" asked Halley.

"Will you give me the string you made from Gezzet's hair? He hides all day in his hut and is no good to the band." The old Boon looked back at Halley, her nose quivering.

"I think I can do that." Halley grinned.

Halley carried a bulging bag to the waste slot in the courtyard behind her apartment building. She didn't need the rest of the hair she had gathered during Trisha's half-price haircut sale. She fingered the strings around her neck. What was she going to do with twenty-two strings twined from the hair of anonymous citizens of Grayplain? She didn't know how to get rid of a living string properly.

The cotton tree in the courtyard, the one she'd gathered cotton from just last year, looked pathetic. Its leaves were curling up, its branches drooping. "That thing needs water!"

On the stairs back up to her apartment, Halley paused. The tree. She'd made a string from its cotton, and used it over and over just a week ago to lure Gezzet into her trap. Had *she* wilted it? Tlakh had talked about using up energy. She must have drawn the power to trap Gezzet from this tree.

She bounded back out into the courtyard, found the gardener's hose, and turned the water on at the tree's base. Droplets splashed up, glinting in the sun's rays. Poor thing, she'd nearly killed it. If she was going to work magic, she'd have to protect her power sources.

The phone's message light blinked in Halley's room when she got home from Trisha's three days later. "Ms. Tuckett," a bored-looking secretary type drawled, "Meng Brothers is pleased to inform you that the planetary quarantine will lift tomorrow. Report to work at your usual time. Thank you." The screen blanked.

It had worked.

As she waited outside Tlakh's compound for the gate to open she could feel Boons—no, Eblekh Zai, she ought to use their real name—watching her from the ghatt trees. When Tlakh opened the gate and welcomed her in, his face twisted in a comical way as he stared at the many strings around her neck.

He ushered her into his hut, away from the staring eyes of his family and apprentices, and she told him the whole story—including Zhettal's offer to make Halley a member of her band.

Tlakh squatted in the dirt, his eyes never leaving her strings. "Khallee, you have much to learn, but not even Pellag, best of my apprentices, could create a new figure as you did. The choice is yours, Khallee. Fekho or Ghuxi. I would be proud to have you in my band."

Business was booming at Trisha's when Halley stopped by a few days later. "Yo, Halley, you got time today?" called Trisha as she walked in.

"Sorry, Trisha, I don't. In fact, I probably won't be in much at all. I've got a new job, and it takes a lot of my time." Grinning, Halley touched the red circles tattooed under her eyes.

About the Author

As writers seem to, **Julia H. West** has held many arcane jobs. When she was a quality control technician for ultrasound heart machines, video recordings of cross sections of her heart were shipped all over the world with the machines. She's also been a genealogical researcher, an office manager, a secretary, a desktop publisher, a digger at an archaeological dig, a quality assurance tech, a webmaster, an aircraft electrician for the Air Force Reserves, and a keyer for the United States Post Office.

Julia loves music, and sings with the Utah Filk Organization (that's not a typo: filk is music of the science fiction and fantasy community). She was a founding member of the local chapter of the Society for Creative Anachronism and still enjoys researching medieval culture. As a member of the Science Fiction and Fantasy Writers of America, she was awarded the Service to SFWA Award. She is a member of the Church of Jesus Christ of Latter-Day Saints (Mormons).

Julia graduated Magna Cum Laude from the University of Utah with a BA in Anthropology. When people asked her what she was going to do with the degree, she'd tell them, "Write science fiction." Many of her stories incorporate fascinating bits of culture she discovered while studying. Julia's website is at http://juliahwest.com

www.ingramcontent.com/pod-product-compliance
Lightning Source LLC
Chambersburg PA
CBHW070636130626
46555CB00006B/2563